consumed by her evening plans. Throughout the day, her nerves grew, making it difficult to concentrate on her work. She reviewed contracts, answered emails, and took calls, but her mind kept drifting to the date she had planned that evening with David, a colleague from the firm.

David was her "safe choice." She didn't expect fireworks but thought starting with someone familiar would be a good way to)avid was an attractive, serious, and polite man, er as terribly predictable. Even so, she clung to nber could work some miracles.

During lunch, Claudia met her best frienc ing's ground floor.

"So, tonight you're starting with your crazy idea?" Laura asked, raising an eyebrow with a playful smile as she stirred her coffee.

"Yep, it's tonight. Six o'clock, at *La Posada del Café*," Claudia replied, trying to sound confident. "David's the first one."

Laura let out a cheerful laugh and raised her cup in a toast.

"To the first of your 24 dates! Here's hoping you find Prince Charming before Christmas!"

Claudia laughed along with her, though a knot in her stomach reminded her how risky her plan really was. But deep inside, a dormant part of her was stirring, excited by the unknown.

The rest of the afternoon dragged on, with piles of paperwork and client calls keeping her occupied. Finally, when the clock struck five-thirty, Claudia shut down her computer, grabbed her things, and took a deep breath before leaving the office. The chilly December evening greeted her, her breath visible in the frosty air as she made her way to the café.

The walk to *La Posada del Café* helped calm her nerves a bit. The streets of Madrid were adorned with Christmas lights, and people bustled past, wrapped in scarves and hats, carrying shopping bags filled with gifts. When she reached the café's entrance, Claudia paused for a moment, peering inside. The warm glow of the lights and the festive decorations brought a smile to her face. The place was nearly empty, save for a few couples tucked into cozy corners.

Miguel, the owner, greeted her with a knowing wink when he saw her come in.

"Claudia, right on time!" he said, motioning toward the table she had reserved by the window, decorated with a small Advent wreath.

"Thanks, Miguel," Claudia replied, removing her coat and draping it over the back of the chair. She sat down and ordered a latte and a slice of apple pie—her favorite.

At exactly six o'clock, the door of the café opened, and David walked in, as punctual as ever. He wore a dark coat and a gray scarf, looking as formal as he did at the office. Claudia smiled at him as he approached with a somewhat stiff smile of his own.

"Hi, Claudia," David greeted her, his tone slightly formal as he took a seat across from her. "I hope I didn't keep you waiting."

"Not at all. You're right on time," Claudia replied, noticing the formality in his tone.

They ordered coffee and cinnamon pastries, attempting to ease into the conversation. They chatted about the holiday decorations, work, and their plans for the season, but the dialogue felt forced. Claudia found herself working hard to keep the conversation interesting, while David seemed unsure how to relax outside of the workplace setting.

After a few minutes of this, Claudia decided to steer the conversation in a more personal direction, hoping to break through his polished exterior.

"So, David... tell me, what's your favorite thing about Christmas?" she asked, leaning slightly forward with a hopeful smile.

David paused, as though the question caught him off guard.

"Well, I guess I like the idea of spending time with family," he finally answered, though without much enthusiasm. "My parents always host a dinner on Christmas Eve. Nothing special, but it's nice."

Claudia nodded, though she felt a pang of disappointment. She was searching for something more—a spark, a passion—but David kept the conversation firmly on a flat, predictable level.

When the date ended, they both stood and said their goodbyes with a handshake that felt far too formal for Claudia's expectations.

"It's been a pleasure, Claudia. Maybe we could do this again sometime if you'd like," David said with a nervous smile.

"Sure... we'll see," Claudia replied, feeling a twinge of guilt for the lack of sincerity in her tone.

David left, and Claudia remained at the table for a few more minutes, savoring the last sip of her coffee as she watched the light snow begin to fall outside the window. Miguel approached her with his usual paternal smile.

The Advent Calendar: A Christmas Love Story

Catalina Doce

December 1st

Claudia Pérez woke up on December 1st determined to change her life. This year, she wouldn't let Christmas catch her alone again, listening to her aunts make the same jokes about her empty love life. At 32 years old, she was a successful lawyer with an enviable career and a seemingly perfect life, but deep down, she felt lonely. The emptiness of not having someone to share those holiday dinners with had become unbearable.

As her alarm buzzed and the first light of dawn filtered through the curtains, Claudia stretched lazily in bed, her eyes landing on the calendar hanging on her wall. Today marked the beginning of her self-declared "advent love calendar," an idea born out of laughter during a dinner with friends a month earlier. Between glasses of wine and jokes, Claudia had promised to find love before December 24th. The goal was simple yet ambitious: 24 dates, one every day, with a different man, always at the same time, in the same place. If she didn't find the right man by Christmas, at least she'd have a host of stories to tell.

Her meeting spot would be *La Posada del Café*, a cozy little coffee shop just a few blocks from her law office. It was her sanctuary, a place where she felt at ease and knew the owners, Miguel and Teresa, an older couple who had turned the café into a warm haven adorned with Christmas decorations. The golden lights and glittering ornaments already brightened the small space, and Claudia felt that, among the aroma of coffee and the festive ambiance, she might find a bit of that holiday magic she longed for.

After showering and dressing for the office, she looked at herself in the mirror with determination. She chose a simple yet elegant red dress, perfectly fitting the festive spirit that had taken over the city. After all, today marked the start of her project to avoid another lonely Christmas.

At the office, the festive mood seemed to have infected everyone but her. Garlands hung from the windows, and a large Christmas tree decorated with red and gold ornaments dominated the reception area. However, Claudia's thoughts were

"So, how did it go?" he asked, his voice warm and curious.

"Not as well as I'd hoped, but not terrible either," Claudia admitted with a shrug.

"Don't worry, it's only the beginning," Miguel said, giving her a reassuring pat on the shoulder. "Christmas magic always takes a little time to show up."

Claudia smiled, grateful for his words, and resolved to stay optimistic. She paid her bill, put on her coat, and stepped out into the cold December night.

As she walked home, she stopped for a moment at the Plaza Mayor, where the enormous Christmas tree glowed with white and gold lights. She stood there for a few minutes, feeling the chill on her cheeks and watching people gather around the tree, laughing and taking pictures.

When she got home, she turned on the lights of the small Christmas tree she'd decorated the night before. Its ornaments sparkled warmly, and Claudia felt as though her apartment, though empty, was filled with a comforting glow. She poured herself a glass of wine, sat on the couch, and opened her planner to review her calendar of dates.

The next day would be more challenging: Álvaro, a fitness trainer she'd met at a work event. He was handsome but also a bit intimidating with his ultra-healthy lifestyle. She smiled to herself, imagining the date, knowing it would likely be an entirely different experience than her evening with David.

Finally, she set her empty glass on the table, turned off the lights, and climbed into bed with her mind filled with anticipation for what December might bring. It had been a long day, but she had the sense that this was just the beginning.

As she closed her eyes, the snow continued to fall gently over the city, blanketing everything in a soft, fresh white. And though she didn't know it yet, Claudia was about to embark on the most exciting journey of her life.

December 2nd

The day after her first date, Claudia woke up with mixed emotions. While her evening with David hadn't been the spark-filled experience she'd hoped for, she felt more motivated than ever to continue her journey. After all, she couldn't expect the first date to be a resounding success; she needed to give her December adventure a real chance.

Winter sunlight brightened the city as Claudia made her way to work. Madrid was filled with Christmas decorations, with lights strung above the streets and shop windows showcasing festive displays. As she walked along the chilly sidewalks, wrapped in her wool coat and red scarf, she couldn't help but smile. Christmas had a way of making her feel optimistic, even when things didn't go as planned.

That morning, Claudia immersed herself in reviewing cases at the office. Work kept her mind occupied, but every now and then, her thoughts drifted to the date she'd scheduled for that evening. Álvaro, the second man on her list, was completely different from David. A fitness trainer, Álvaro was someone who dedicated his life to health and wellness. While he was undeniably attractive and full of energy, Claudia worried the conversation might revolve entirely around diets and exercise. Still, she was determined to give him a fair chance.

During lunch, she shared her thoughts with Laura, who, as always, was ready to hear every detail.

"A personal trainer?" Laura asked, raising an eyebrow as she sipped her tea. "And how did you meet him?"

"I met him at a charity event organized by the office a few months ago," Claudia explained, recalling Álvaro's impeccable outfit and his passionate speech on healthy lifestyles. "He's one of those guys who seems to live at the gym, you know... but he seemed nice enough."

Laura laughed, amused.

"Well, it sounds like this date will at least be interesting. What's the plan?"

"We're meeting at the same café at six," Claudia said with a shrug. "I like keeping everything in one place—it makes logistics easier. Plus, *La Posada del Café* has that perfect Christmas vibe."

Laura nodded in agreement and raised her cup in a mock toast.

"To date number two. Here's hoping there's a bit more chemistry this time!"

Claudia smiled, though she wasn't entirely sure what to expect. Whatever happened, she was determined to enjoy the experience, and who knew? Maybe Álvaro would turn out to be a pleasant surprise.

The day passed quickly between meetings and legal documents. When the clock struck five-thirty, Claudia gathered her things, feeling that familiar knot of nerves return to her stomach. She left the office, adjusting her scarf around her neck as she walked toward the café. The cold air bit at her cheeks, but the anticipation gave her a strange sense of warmth.

She arrived a few minutes early, and Miguel, the owner of *La Posada del Café*, greeted her with a knowing smile.

"Back again, Claudia?" he said, gesturing to the table by the window he'd reserved for her. "This must be your second date, right?"

Claudia nodded, smiling.

"That's right, Miguel. Let's see if tonight brings better luck."

"I'm sure it will," he replied, giving her a wink before retreating to the counter.

Claudia removed her coat and draped it over the back of her chair, ordering a chai latte while she waited for Álvaro. She didn't have to wait long. At exactly six o'clock, the door to the café opened with a soft chime, and Álvaro stepped in, radiating energy and confidence. He wore a tailored wool coat and a black beanie, looking as though he'd just finished a workout. Claudia waved to him, trying to appear relaxed.

"Hi, Claudia!" Álvaro said warmly, flashing a wide smile as he approached the table. "It's great to see you. The city looks amazing this time of year, doesn't it?"

"Yes, Madrid has a special charm during Christmas," Claudia replied, grateful that the conversation started naturally.

Álvaro ordered a protein shake, which made Claudia suppress a small laugh. It wasn't the typical drink for a cozy café in the middle of winter, but it didn't surprise her.

The conversation began lightly, and in the first few minutes, Claudia realized that Álvaro was indeed a friendly person. He spoke with enthusiasm about his work, his clients, and how he'd helped people transform their lives through fitness. Claudia listened attentively, even though the subject wasn't entirely her cup of tea.

"What about you?" Álvaro asked, steering the conversation toward her. "Tell me more about your work. I know you're a lawyer, but I've never really understood what you do exactly."

Claudia briefly explained her specialty in corporate law, trying to make it sound as engaging as possible. Álvaro seemed genuinely interested, though he admitted he preferred to "avoid legal problems whenever possible." Claudia laughed, feeling herself relax a little more.

However, as the conversation progressed, she noticed that Álvaro had a tendency to steer everything back to fitness. He talked about his eating habits, the workout routines he designed for his clients, the supplements he took, and the benefits of a stress-free life. Claudia tried to stay engaged, but she soon realized they lived in completely different worlds. As he passionately extolled the virtues of a keto diet, she found herself longing for another slice of apple pie.

The conversation finally shifted to more personal topics, and Claudia tried to explore Álvaro's emotional side. She wanted to know if there was more to him than muscles and protein shakes.

"So, Álvaro, tell me... how do you usually spend Christmas?" Claudia asked, hoping his answer would reveal a warmer side.

He shrugged, as if Christmas didn't hold much meaning for him.

"Well, honestly, I don't do anything special. I usually train in the morning, you know, to stay in shape even during the holidays. Then I spend some time with my family, but I'm not a big fan of holiday feasts. I prefer to stick to my routine," he replied with a satisfied smile. "For me, Christmas is just another opportunity to stay disciplined."

Claudia felt a pang of disappointment. She knew Álvaro's healthy lifestyle was important to him, but she had hoped to uncover a side of him that valued the warmth and joy of the holidays. She tried to steer the conversation in another direction, but Álvaro always found a way to bring it back to exercise and nutrition.

When the waiter brought over a tray of complimentary gingerbread cookies, Claudia decided to test his reaction.

"Oh, look! Gingerbread cookies, my favorite," she said with a smile. "Want to try one?"

Álvaro looked at her as if she'd offered him poison instead of a sweet treat.

"No, thanks. I don't eat sugar," he said, raising his hands in polite refusal.

Claudia laughed, trying to hide her frustration, and picked up a cookie for herself, savoring every bite of the delicious blend of cinnamon and ginger. It became clear that their differences were irreconcilable, but she decided to stay positive until the end of the date.

The conversation continued pleasantly but stayed superficial until they finished their drinks. Although the evening wasn't uncomfortable, Claudia knew there was no special connection with Álvaro. She thanked him for his company, and he, with his signature confident smile, invited her to join him at the gym one day.

"I mean it, Claudia," Álvaro said as they stood to leave. "You should come train with me sometime. I think you'd love it—it's a great way to balance work and exercise."

Claudia smiled, even though she knew there wouldn't be a second date.

"I'll think about it, Álvaro. Thanks for the offer and for tonight."

Álvaro leaned in for a kiss on the cheek before leaving, leaving behind a faint trail of cologne and a somewhat blurry impression in her mind. Claudia sighed, feeling a mix of relief and mild disappointment. He wasn't what she was looking for, but at least the date had been a learning experience.

As Miguel came over to collect the cups, Claudia couldn't help but laugh softly.

"This one wasn't your ideal match either, was he?" Miguel asked with a knowing tone.

"Definitely not," Claudia replied, shaking her head. "He's very nice, but we have nothing in common. For him, Christmas is just another excuse to work out harder."

Miguel chuckled and offered her a piece of wisdom.

"Sometimes you have to meet the wrong people to be sure of what you're really looking for, don't you think?"

Claudia nodded, knowing he was right. Each date brought her one step closer to understanding what she truly wanted. As she paid her bill, Miguel winked at her.

"I'll see you tomorrow, Claudia. Let's hope the next date has a bit more magic."

She smiled, grateful for his constant support, and stepped out into the cold night. Slowly, she walked back to her apartment, enjoying the fresh air and the quiet calm of the city as it wrapped itself in a light dusting of snow.

At home, Claudia turned on the lights of her Christmas tree and settled on the couch with a glass of wine. She opened her planner and checked the next name on her calendar: Sergio, the philosophy professor.

Claudia smiled to herself, intrigued. She knew Sergio would be a completely different experience, and after her date with Álvaro, she felt ready for something more intellectual and reflective.

Finally, she turned off the lights and climbed into bed, feeling more hopeful than ever. With every date, she was discovering not only more about others but also about herself.

And while Christmas crept closer, the magic of the season seemed to be unfolding around her, slowly but surely.

December 3rd

Claudia's alarm buzzed at 7:00 a.m., and her first thought was about the date from the night before. While it had been a little disappointing, she'd learned something important about herself: she needed someone with a warmer personality, someone who shared her passion for life beyond workouts and strict diets. Álvaro had been charming but shallow. Claudia was definitely looking for something deeper.

As she got ready for work, her thoughts turned to the date she had planned for that evening. The third man on her list was Sergio, a philosophy professor she'd met briefly during a creative writing course a few months earlier. Sergio was an intriguing figure: messy hair, dark-rimmed glasses, and a calm demeanor that exuded quiet confidence. She wasn't sure what to expect from him, but something about his measured voice and thoughtful responses had caught her attention. Tonight, she was looking for a meaningful and honest conversation—something that might allow her to connect with someone on a deeper level.

The day at the office passed quickly, filled with contracts and meetings. Over lunch, Laura asked about Sergio with her trademark curiosity.

"So, the intellectual, huh?" Laura teased with a playful grin, poking at her salad.

"Yep, Sergio. He's a philosophy professor. Last time we spoke, he spent half an hour talking to me about Aristotle's definition of happiness," Claudia replied, laughing at the memory.

Laura gasped dramatically, raising her hand in mock distress.

"Oh, Aristotle and happiness! I hope he doesn't recite Socrates in Ancient Greek tonight..."

Claudia joined in the laughter, but deep down, she hoped Sergio would be different from her first two dates. She wanted to believe there were still men who could hold an honest and engaging conversation without any pretense. After lunch, she returned to her desk with renewed energy, curious about what the evening might bring.

By 5:30, she packed up her things and left the office, mentally preparing herself for the date. Madrid was especially beautiful that evening, with Christmas lights twinkling everywhere and a pleasant chill in the air that made it feel like the holidays were just around the corner.

When Claudia arrived at *La Posada del Café*, Miguel greeted her with his usual humor.

"Claudia, I get the feeling you're turning my café into a dating hub," he said, chuckling as he motioned to her usual table by the window.

"I promise not to cause any trouble, Miguel," Claudia replied with a smile. "Tonight's the third date. I'm practically an expert at this now."

Miguel nodded and gave her an encouraging look before heading back to the counter. Claudia ordered a hot chocolate to calm her nerves, and just a few minutes after six, the door opened and Sergio walked in. He wore a long black coat and a gray wool scarf. With a small, shy smile, he greeted her and removed his gloves as he sat down across from her.

"Hi, Claudia. It's nice to see you," he said in his usual calm tone.

"Hi, Sergio. I'm glad you could make it," she replied, smiling as he settled into his seat.

Sergio ordered a black coffee, and they began talking. At first, the conversation was polite and centered around light topics like the weather and the city's holiday decorations. But Claudia noticed something different about Sergio from the start: he seemed genuinely interested in what she had to say. He asked her about her work, her thoughts on city life, and her favorite Christmas traditions. She felt at ease with him, as though she were talking to an old friend.

Soon, their discussion took a more philosophical turn. When Claudia asked Sergio why he'd chosen to study philosophy, he smiled thoughtfully before answering.

"I've always been fascinated by questions without answers," he said, his voice carrying a quiet passion. "For me, philosophy is the pursuit of truth—but not an absolute truth. I like the idea of exploring, of never settling for one explanation. Especially during the holiday season, I find it's a perfect time to reflect on that. People get caught up in the perfection of Christmas, but in reality, we're all still searching for something... something we're not even sure exists."

Claudia felt the conversation shift into intriguing territory. It was exactly what she had hoped for: an exchange of ideas instead of shallow small talk. She decided to follow his train of thought, curious to learn more about his perspective.

"So, do you think Christmas is about searching for something that doesn't exist?" she asked, her expression playful yet inquisitive as she took a sip of her hot chocolate.

Sergio looked at her, clearly pleased by her engagement with the topic.

"Not exactly," he replied. "I think Christmas reflects what we desire—what we believe happiness should look like. We decorate our homes, buy gifts, prepare special meals... but ultimately, it's all symbolic. What we're really searching for isn't material—it's connection, warmth, a sense of belonging. And for many of us, we don't quite know how to find it."

Claudia nodded, reflecting on her own reasons for embarking on this "advent calendar" of dates. After all, she too was searching for something deeper than just a dinner companion for Christmas Eve. Sergio seemed to be right—Christmas was, for many, an excuse to look for something lasting and meaningful.

The next hour flew by as they discussed their favorite holiday traditions, movies, and family customs. Sergio's passion for books, stories, and the small details of life impressed Claudia. She appreciated his unique way of looking at the world, always through a lens of curiosity and reflection. However, there were moments when the conversation became a bit too abstract, and Claudia found herself struggling to keep up. Still, she couldn't deny that she enjoyed their time together.

When their drinks were finished, Sergio suggested taking a short walk to the nearby Christmas market. Claudia hesitated for a moment before agreeing, intrigued by his proposal. They bundled up and strolled through the festive streets of Madrid, passing shop windows filled with holiday treats and small stalls selling ornaments and sweets. The air was crisp, and the glow of the Christmas lights gave the city an almost magical feel.

At the market, they stopped to admire handmade crafts and a small carousel spinning in the square. Sergio bought a cone of roasted chestnuts and offered to share them with Claudia. She accepted, savoring the warmth of the treat as they continued to walk and talk.

Their evening ended in a quiet plaza, where a giant Christmas tree stood glowing with white and gold lights. Couples gathered around it, laughing and taking photos. Claudia and Sergio stopped to admire the scene, both seemingly lost in their own thoughts.

As much as Claudia appreciated the evening, she realized that, while Sergio was fascinating and kind, there wasn't a romantic spark between them. He was someone she could talk to for hours, but she didn't feel the connection she was hoping for.

Sergio seemed to sense it too. After a brief silence, he smiled warmly.

"I'm glad we got to spend this time together, Claudia. It's been an interesting evening," he said, his tone both grateful and lightly resigned.

Claudia smiled back, feeling the same way.

"Yes, it has. I've enjoyed talking to you, Sergio. You're a very interesting person."

They parted with a friendly hug, and Claudia watched as Sergio walked away into the night. She lingered by the tree for a few moments, letting the chilly air clear her thoughts.

Back at her apartment, Claudia turned on her Christmas tree lights and settled onto the couch with a glass of wine. As she wrote her reflections on the date in her journal, she acknowledged that, while she hadn't found romance with Sergio, she had learned something about herself.

She checked her calendar: December 4th—Jorge, the bohemian artist. Claudia smiled to herself, intrigued by what the next evening might bring.

As she drifted off to sleep, she felt hopeful, knowing that each experience was bringing her closer to understanding what she truly wanted—and perhaps, to the person who might share it with her.

December 4th

The December sun barely peeked over the buildings of Madrid as Claudia woke up. The soft light filled her bedroom, and the crisp breeze seeping through the window reminded her that winter was in full swing. Her date with Sergio had been enriching, but the lack of a romantic connection left her feeling reflective. Claudia knew she wasn't just looking for someone to hold a good conversation with; she needed a spark—something that could light her heart.

As she prepared for the day, her thoughts turned to her next date. Jorge, the fourth man on her list, was a bohemian artist she'd met at an art exhibition in Malasaña the year before. Jorge was tall and lean, with a deliberately disheveled style that gave off an air of effortless creativity. He was the kind of man who always wore a long, colorful scarf, spoke passionately about his work, and seemed to exist in his own world of abstract ideas and emotions. Claudia couldn't help but feel curious about how the evening would unfold with someone so vastly different from anyone else she'd dated so far.

The morning at the office was particularly hectic, with year-end cases piling up as everyone scrambled to wrap things up before the holidays. Amid the whirlwind of contracts and client calls, Claudia found her thoughts drifting to the night ahead. She wasn't sure if Jorge would be a disaster or a delightful surprise, but she was certain he wouldn't be boring.

During lunch, Laura listened attentively as Claudia shared her thoughts.

"So, what do you know about this guy?" Laura asked, her eyes sparkling with curiosity.

"Not much, really. Jorge's a painter, and, well... he lives in his own world," Claudia replied with a shrug. "The last time we talked, he spent thirty minutes explaining the symbolism of his colors and shapes. But honestly, I don't know much else about him. He's... different."

Laura laughed, clearly entertained.

"Sounds like an adventure. Just remember not to get lost in his stories. Artists can be... unpredictable!"

Claudia chuckled, but Laura's warning lingered in her mind. This date could either be a complete disaster or one of the most memorable evenings of her life. Either way, she was ready for the unexpected.

At 5:30, Claudia left her desk and headed to *La Posada del Café*, her scarf wrapped tightly around her neck. The city streets glowed with festive lights, and the air carried the sweet scent of roasted chestnuts from nearby market stalls. Claudia felt a strange energy in the air, a mix of nervousness and excitement.

When she arrived at the café, Miguel greeted her with his usual warm smile, though with a hint of mischief.

"There's a different sparkle in your eyes tonight, Claudia," he observed as he escorted her to her table by the window. "Expecting something special?"

Claudia laughed, draping her coat over the chair.

"I'm expecting... something different, yes," she replied cryptically. She ordered a fruit tea to calm her nerves and waited, arriving her usual ten minutes early.

At six o'clock sharp, the café door opened, and Jorge strode in. He wore a tilted beret, a patched wool jacket, and, of course, the vibrant scarf Claudia remembered. His grin was wide and open, as if seeing Claudia felt like reuniting with an old friend.

"Claudia!" he exclaimed, approaching her table with enthusiasm. "What a joy to see you!"

"Hi, Jorge. I'm glad you came," Claudia replied, smiling as he gave her an unprompted, warm hug.

Jorge settled into the chair across from her and ordered a black coffee with a touch of cinnamon. From the moment he began speaking, Claudia realized that Jorge wasn't like anyone she'd ever dated.

The conversation was chaotic and enchanting, jumping from one topic to another without much logical flow. Jorge talked passionately about his latest artistic projects, describing colors, emotions, and textures with a vividness that painted pictures in Claudia's mind.

"Colors are like living emotions," he explained, gesturing wildly with his hands. "This year, I've been obsessed with green and red. Green symbolizes hope—but not a simple hope. It's a hope that fights, that grows through uncertainty. And red... ah, red! It's passion, love, and rage all at once. It's Christmas, with all its contradictions. Don't you find that fascinating?"

Claudia listened, simultaneously captivated and amused by Jorge's exuberance. His personality was larger than life, and though she wasn't sure if there was a romantic connection, she couldn't deny that she was thoroughly entertained.

They talked about art, Christmas, and city life, with Jorge often interrupting himself to ask Claudia a question or comment on a passing thought. She appreciated that, despite his whirlwind energy, he seemed genuinely interested in her answers.

"Do you believe in destiny, Claudia?" he asked suddenly, his expression playful and curious.

She paused, caught off guard.

"I don't know... I've never really thought about it," she admitted. "I guess I don't believe in a fixed destiny, but I do think life presents us with opportunities. Do you believe in destiny?"

Jorge leaned forward, resting his elbows on the table.

"I believe destiny is like a painting in constant flux," he said, his voice filled with conviction. "Sometimes, all it takes is one brushstroke to transform the entire canvas. And I feel like Christmas is often one of those brushstrokes. Don't you think?"

Claudia couldn't help but smile at the metaphor, even if she wasn't sure how much of it she truly believed. There was something intoxicating about Jorge's way of looking at the world.

When their drinks were finished, Jorge surprised Claudia with an unexpected invitation.

"I have an idea. Would you like to see my studio? It's just a few blocks from here," he suggested, his eyes twinkling with excitement. "Only if you have the time, of course."

Claudia hesitated but found herself unable to resist her curiosity. She nodded, and they left the café together.

The walk to his studio took them through narrow, cobblestoned streets lined with Christmas lights and bustling with holiday shoppers. The air was cold, but Claudia barely noticed as Jorge talked animatedly about his art and life in Madrid.

When they arrived, Jorge led her into a small, cluttered space filled with canvases, paintbrushes, and jars of vibrant pigments. A large window overlooked the city, glowing softly in the winter night.

"This is where the magic happens," Jorge declared, spreading his arms like a ringmaster.

Claudia laughed, feeling as though she'd stepped into another world. She wandered through the studio, admiring unfinished paintings and half-sketched ideas. Jorge handed her a brush and grinned.

"Go on. Add a stroke to this piece. I insist—it'll be our collaboration."

After some hesitation, Claudia dipped the brush into a deep red paint and added a bold curve to the canvas. Jorge clapped his hands dramatically.

"Perfect! Now this painting is ours," he declared with mock solemnity.

The night ended far later than Claudia had anticipated. Jorge walked her to her apartment building, his energy never faltering. As they said goodbye, Claudia realized that, while the date had been thrilling and fun, there hadn't been a romantic spark. Jorge's world was fascinating, but it felt like a place she could only visit, not stay.

"I'd love for you to come by the studio again," Jorge said, giving her a warm hug. "Next time, we'll paint something together."

"Maybe I will," Claudia replied sincerely. "Thank you for tonight, Jorge. It was... unforgettable."

Back in her apartment, Claudia poured herself a glass of wine and reflected on the night. Jorge had brought a burst of color into her life, but she knew he wasn't the one. Still, she felt grateful for the experience and the reminder that stepping out of her comfort zone could be rewarding.

She checked her calendar: December 5th—Pablo, the arrogant banker.

Claudia sighed, already imagining the challenge the next evening might bring. But for now, she let herself bask in the warmth of the night's adventure, knowing that each step in her journey was teaching her more about herself and what she truly wanted.

December 5th

The sound of her alarm pulled Claudia from a deep sleep. It was December 5th, and as the soft morning light crept through her curtains, she lingered under the blankets for a few extra minutes, reflecting on the night before. Jorge, the bohemian artist, had brought a splash of color and chaos into her life. While she appreciated his energy and creative world, she knew it wasn't what she was looking for. There had been no spark, no true connection—only a brief visit to a world she couldn't fully inhabit.

Claudia pushed herself out of bed, opened the curtains, and stared out at a city still wrapped in the quiet of an early winter morning. Today's date brought a new challenge. Pablo, the fifth man on her list, was a banker she'd met at a corporate networking event months ago. Her impression of him was that he enjoyed talking about his accomplishments, expensive possessions, and his next exotic vacation. Still, Claudia had decided to give him a chance. Maybe there was more to Pablo than what he chose to show on the surface.

At the office, the morning passed quickly, with contracts and client meetings keeping her busy. By lunchtime, Laura was already teasing her about the upcoming date.

"So, tonight it's the banker?" Laura asked, her grin mischievous as she stabbed at her salad.

"Yes, Pablo," Claudia replied with a dramatic sigh. "The last time we spoke, he couldn't stop talking about his investments and his new sports car."

Laura laughed and nudged her playfully.

"Well, don't write him off just yet. Maybe there's a softer side to him you haven't seen."

"I hope so," Claudia said, managing a smile. "But I have a feeling this date is going to be... interesting."

When lunchtime ended, Claudia returned to her desk, determined to approach the evening with an open mind. Life was full of surprises, after all, and perhaps Pablo had hidden depths waiting to be discovered.

At 5:30, Claudia shut down her computer and left the office. She walked briskly through the streets of Madrid, the chilly December air biting at her cheeks. The city glowed with festive lights, and the scent of roasted chestnuts wafted from street vendors. She breathed deeply, hoping the fresh air would calm her nerves.

When she arrived at *La Posada del Café*, Miguel greeted her warmly and handed her a steaming cup of her favorite tea.

"Here you go, Claudia. Tea to settle the nerves," he said with a smile, placing the cup on the table by the window.

Claudia smiled in return, sitting down and mentally preparing for whatever the night might bring. She didn't have to wait long. At precisely six o'clock, the door to the café opened with a chime, and Pablo walked in. He was immaculately dressed in a tailored camel coat, leather gloves, and a silk scarf draped effortlessly over his shoulders. With a confident smile, he approached the table and greeted Claudia with a kiss on each cheek.

"Claudia, it's so good to see you," he said, pulling out his chair with an air of self-assurance.

"Hi, Pablo. Thanks for coming," Claudia replied, offering him a polite smile.

Pablo ordered an espresso—"the best in the house," he declared—and wasted no time diving into a monologue about his latest successes. He spoke of his recent promotion, a new luxury apartment he'd bought in the heart of Madrid, and his upcoming ski trip to the Alps for the holidays. Claudia listened politely, nodding at appropriate moments, but found it difficult to insert herself into the conversation.

"You know, the other day I closed an incredible deal with one of the bank's most important clients," Pablo said, gesturing dramatically. "It was a multimillion-euro operation. Not just anyone could have pulled it off, but it's all about strategy, you see."

Claudia stifled a sigh, realizing that Pablo seemed far more interested in impressing her than getting to know her. She decided to try steering the conversation toward something more personal.

"That's impressive, Pablo. But tell me, how do you usually spend Christmas?" she asked, hoping to uncover a warmer side of him.

Pablo shrugged casually, as if the question didn't carry much weight.

"Oh, the usual. Family dinners, a few corporate events. But honestly, I prefer to do something exclusive. This year, I'll be skiing in the Alps. I'm not really into all that traditional Christmas stuff," he said with a smirk.

Claudia nodded, feeling a pang of disappointment. There was nothing wrong with enjoying luxurious vacations, but his dismissive tone made her wonder if they had anything in common.

As the conversation continued, Pablo's focus remained firmly on himself. He offered unsolicited financial advice, suggesting Claudia diversify her investments and take advantage of "amazing opportunities in the market." While Claudia appreciated his enthusiasm, she couldn't shake the feeling that he wasn't truly interested in her or her opinions.

"Claudia, I think you should consider letting your money work for you," Pablo said at one point, his voice filled with the confidence of someone used to being listened to. "I could even help you with some pointers, if you're interested."

Claudia bit her tongue, resisting the urge to reply with sarcasm. Instead, she tried one last time to redirect the conversation.

"So, what makes you happy, Pablo? Beyond work, I mean. What really excites you?" she asked, hoping to uncover a glimpse of vulnerability.

For a moment, Pablo seemed caught off guard. He stared into his espresso cup as if searching for the answer. Then, with a smile that felt more rehearsed than sincere, he replied, "Well, I like winning. I'm passionate about succeeding at whatever I do. I guess happiness for me is standing on top, enjoying everything I've worked hard for. What about you, Claudia?"

Claudia paused, her thoughts swirling. How could she explain that her idea of happiness was so different from his? She wanted connection, warmth, and the joy found in small, meaningful moments—not a constant chase for the next victory.

"For me, Christmas is about sharing moments with the people I love," she finally said. "I enjoy the little things, like baking cookies with my mom or watching holiday movies under a blanket."

Pablo nodded politely, but she could tell her answer didn't resonate with him.

When the date finally ended, Claudia felt a sense of relief. Pablo insisted on paying the bill, which might have been a kind gesture if it hadn't come with an air of superiority.

"It's been an interesting evening, Claudia," Pablo said as they stood by the door. "Maybe we can do this again sometime, if you'd like."

Claudia forced a polite smile and nodded, though she knew there wouldn't be a second date.

"Thank you, Pablo. Have a good night," she said as he kissed her on the cheek and walked away, his expensive coat swaying in the chilly breeze.

Claudia lingered outside the café, watching him disappear into the night. She felt a mixture of disappointment and exhaustion—not because the date had gone poorly, but because it had reminded her how much she valued authenticity.

Back in her apartment, Claudia turned on the Christmas tree lights, but the usual warmth they radiated failed to soothe her. She poured herself a glass of wine and curled up on the couch, wrapped in her favorite blanket. She replayed the evening in her mind, searching for something positive to take away from her date with Pablo, but all she could recall was the feeling of disconnection and the certainty that a man like him wasn't what she was looking for.

She reached for her journal and began writing about the experience, acknowledging that, while Pablo wasn't the right man for her, the date had taught her an important lesson. She promised herself not to settle, not to lose sight of what she truly wanted: someone who shared her passion for life, her love for the little things, and the ability to laugh even during life's toughest moments.

As she finished writing, her phone buzzed with a calendar notification: December 6th – Daniel, the charming musician.Claudia smiled faintly. The next date sounded far more promising. A musician was exactly what she needed right now: someone creative, someone soulful, someone who could share an evening of genuine laughter and, if she was lucky, leave a melody in her heart.

She turned off the lights, closed her eyes, and let the day's exhaustion carry her away, hoping that her next encounter would be different—hoping that, at last, the magic of Christmas would begin to shine in her life.

December 6th

Claudia woke up on December 6th with a renewed sense of hope. After the disappointing date with Pablo, she knew she had to move forward and keep faith in her Christmas quest. There were still plenty of dates ahead, and tonight she had one with a musician. Not just any musician, but Daniel, a charismatic guitarist she had met months ago at an indie music concert in a small bar in Lavapiés. Daniel was a man with an easy smile, dark eyes, and a soft voice that lingered in memory like a catchy melody. Claudia had a feeling this date would be different, and she decided to trust her intuition.

As she got ready for work, she carefully selected her outfit: a casual yet cozy dress paired with a cream-colored sweater and a wool scarf that added a wintry touch. She wanted to look presentable but not like she had tried too hard. Her reflection in the mirror smiled back at her nervously. She knew this date had the potential to be special—or at the very least, more enjoyable than the last one.

The day at the office was more relaxed than usual. The holiday spirit had eased tensions, and Laura, her ever-reliable confidante, encouraged her during their coffee break.

"So, tonight's the date with the musician?" Laura asked, stirring her cappuccino with a tiny silver spoon.

"Yes, Daniel. He's an incredible guitarist and seems like a good person… you know, someone laid-back," Claudia replied, trying not to sound too enthusiastic.

"I love it," Laura said with a knowing grin. "I think it's just what you need after last night's date. Musicians always have something… special. Maybe he'll surprise you."

Claudia nodded, knowing Laura was right. There was something about creative people that drew her in, and she needed a date with someone who could embrace spontaneity and enjoy the little things—something entirely different from the rigid formality she had felt with Pablo.

As the evening fell, Claudia left the office and made her way to *La Posada del Café*. She walked slowly, savoring the crisp air and the smell of roasted chestnuts wafting from street vendors. That night, the city's Christmas lights seemed brighter, the breeze less cold, as if everything conspired to make the evening magical.

When she arrived at the café, Miguel greeted her from behind the counter with a warm, familiar smile.

"Claudia, you've got a special sparkle in your eyes tonight," he said as he prepared her favorite drink: a chai latte, perfect for chilly evenings.

"It's just that... I feel like this date might be different, Miguel. You know, sometimes I think of this quest as playing a song. Some notes don't hit the mark, but I keep searching for the right melody," Claudia replied, feeling a bit poetic.

Miguel nodded as he placed her cup on her usual table by the window. At precisely six o'clock, the door swung open, and Daniel walked in with a wide, carefree smile. He wore a worn leather jacket, dark jeans, and an emerald-green scarf that gave him a bohemian air. Slung over his back was a guitar case, making him look like a wandering musician fresh off the road.

"Claudia!" he called out enthusiastically, raising a hand in greeting. "Sorry if I'm cutting it close—I came straight from rehearsal."

"Don't worry, you're right on time," she replied, smiling as he took the seat across from her.

Daniel ordered a latte and started talking about his day in a way that felt effortless and engaging. Unlike her previous dates, Claudia felt an immediate flow in their conversation, as if they had known each other for years. Daniel had a unique way of holding eye contact, truly listening, and making every topic seem interesting, whether it was his latest band rehearsal or childhood memories of growing up in a small coastal town.

The conversation soon grew lively, and Claudia discovered a humorous side to Daniel she hadn't expected. He shared lighthearted jokes, funny anecdotes about his bandmates, and wasn't afraid to laugh at himself. He seemed to relish life as it came, without worrying too much about the future—a refreshing contrast to the seriousness Claudia had felt with Pablo.

They talked about music, the songs that shaped their lives, and what being a musician meant to him.

"I've always thought music is like Christmas," Daniel said at one point, a nostalgic smile on his face. "It's the one thing that, when it arrives, transforms everything around it. It can make you feel sadder or happier, but it always changes something. I guess that's why I love playing so much this time of year."

Delighted by the comparison, Claudia asked about his favorite Christmas songs, and their conversation shifted to a spirited debate about holiday classics. As they talked, Daniel pulled out a small notebook and started sketching on the last page.

"I always do this during interesting conversations," he said, looking up with a smile. "It's my way of capturing the moment."

Claudia watched him sketch with curiosity, enjoying every detail. She noticed in him a mix of simplicity and complexity that intrigued her, and for the first time since beginning her "advent dating calendar," she felt truly in sync with someone.

When their conversation turned to holiday plans, Daniel asked if she'd like to hear one of his new songs. Surprised and flattered, Claudia agreed eagerly. Without saying more, Daniel walked to the counter to speak with Miguel. The café owner, ever the accomplice, dimmed the main lights, leaving only the twinkling Christmas lights decorating the walls and the tree in the corner.

Daniel returned to their table, removed his guitar from its case, and sat on a stool near the window. The guitar looked well-worn, as though it had seen many stories. He adjusted the strings and glanced at Claudia with a look of playful complicity.

"This is a song I wrote recently. It's about the magic of small things—those we often overlook until it's too late. I hope you like it," he said, and began to play.

Claudia sat in silence, moved by Daniel's soft, resonant voice. The melody was simple yet beautiful, filled with warm notes that seemed to envelop the café in an intimate atmosphere. The lyrics spoke of beauty in imperfection, of finding value in the ordinary. Claudia felt a part of her heart, long closed off by fear of failure, begin to open.

When Daniel finished, the café filled with applause. Claudia, still moved, smiled and leaned in to give him a heartfelt hug.

"That was beautiful, Daniel. Truly, thank you," she said, feeling her words fall short.

"Thank you for listening. It's always better to play when you know someone's really there, on the other side," he replied with a warm smile.

Back at their table, the atmosphere had shifted. There was a new sense of connection, one neither of them tried to hide. Claudia felt that, for the first time in her Christmas dating experiment, she was experiencing more than just a pleasant conversation—it was something real.

When the date ended, Daniel walked her to the door, his guitar slung over his shoulder and a smile that seemed to light up the night. The cold air wrapped around them, but neither seemed to notice as they strolled through streets adorned with holiday lights.

"This has been an amazing night, Claudia," Daniel said, stopping near a small Christmas tree decorated in a nearby plaza.

"It has. Thank you for… everything. The music, the company…" she replied, sincerity flowing from her heart.

They shared a quiet moment, standing still and feeling the weight of the evening. Claudia realized she wanted to know more about Daniel, to explore this connection, but she also didn't want to rush. Memories of past dates where the lack of chemistry had left her disheartened kept her cautious.

Daniel, perhaps sensing her hesitation, smiled warmly.

"If you ever want to do this again, you know where to find me," he said, raising a hand in a friendly, genuine gesture.

Claudia nodded, feeling a mix of hope and caution. They said goodbye with a long, warm hug, and then he walked away, disappearing into the shadows of the Madrid night. Claudia lingered in the plaza, gazing at the twinkling lights on the tree, feeling something had shifted inside her. She didn't know if Daniel was "the one," but there was something about him that made her want to know more, to explore further.

When Claudia got home, she kicked off her boots and coat and sank into the sofa, staring at the Christmas lights she had put up in late November. Pouring herself a glass of wine, she pulled out her journal and began writing about the night, capturing every detail—from Daniel's song to the way he had looked at her while they talked. Unlike other dates, there was nothing she wanted to forget or change. Everything had been perfectly imperfect.

She realized she hadn't felt the usual pressure to find "the one." With Daniel, she had been able to relax and enjoy the moment without worrying about what came next. Maybe, she thought, that's how love should feel: something that flows naturally, without complications or impossible expectations.

As she turned off the lights and got ready for bed, her phone buzzed with a calendar notification: December 7th – Luis, the shy guy. Claudia smiled, knowing the adventure was far from over. Though she hadn't found her great love yet, she felt closer than ever to something real.

Snuggling under the blankets, she closed her eyes, letting the memory of Daniel's music lull her to sleep, dreaming of new melodies and future encounters under the holiday lights.

December 7th

Claudia woke up on December 7th with Daniel's music still echoing in her mind. The night had been magical, filled with laughter and a deep sense of connection. While there hadn't been a romantic crescendo, something about the evening left her feeling hopeful. She wasn't sure if Daniel was "the one," but for the first time in weeks, she had felt a genuine bond with someone.

As she got ready for work, her thoughts drifted to her upcoming date that evening. Luis, a programmer she'd met at a networking event over a year ago, was next on her schedule. Her impression of Luis was that of a reserved man, almost uncomfortable in social settings, with an intelligence that sometimes felt overwhelming. It was a stark contrast to Daniel's charismatic energy, and Claudia wasn't sure how the evening would unfold. Still, she had learned not to judge anyone too quickly. Her date with the bohemian artist Jorge had taught her that first impressions were often misleading.

At the office, Laura was her usual supportive self, but Claudia felt a subtle shift in their dynamic. Her friend asked about the date with Daniel, and while Claudia spoke enthusiastically, she was also candid about her uncertainties. She wasn't sure if what she felt was enough or if she was simply idealizing the evening. With many more dates ahead, the constant uncertainty was beginning to wear on her.

As the afternoon progressed, Claudia grew increasingly anxious about her date with Luis. She knew it wouldn't be as effortless as the previous night, but she was determined not to dismiss anyone without giving them a fair chance.

The clock struck 5:30 as Claudia left the office. Stepping out into the crisp December air, she wrapped herself tightly in her coat and made her way to La Posada del Café. The chill in the air carried the promise of Christmas, and the golden lights adorning the streets seemed to glow with a special warmth. Claudia took a deep breath, trying to calm her nerves. This date felt like a test of her patience, one she wasn't entirely confident she would pass.

When she arrived at the café, Miguel greeted her with his usual cheerful smile and a reassuring nod.

"Another date tonight?" he asked, placing a cup of ginger tea on the table she had come to think of as her "date table."

"Yes, and I have a strange feeling about it," Claudia admitted, smiling with a mix of anxiety and resignation.

Miguel patted her shoulder before stepping away, leaving her staring at her reflection in the window. She tried to convince herself that everything would turn out fine.

At exactly six o'clock, the door swung open gently, and Luis walked into the café, his head slightly bowed and his expression nervous. He was dressed casually in a dark gray sweater, jeans, and a simple coat. Though understated, his appearance had an air of sincerity that Claudia found instantly endearing.

Luis spotted her and raised a shy hand in greeting. She smiled and motioned for him to come over. He sat down across from her, awkwardly removing his coat, and offered a nervous smile.

"Hi, Claudia. I hope I'm not too early," he said, his soft voice almost hesitant to disturb the cozy atmosphere of the café.

"Not at all! You're right on time," Claudia replied warmly, hoping to ease the tension.

Luis ordered a black coffee, and their conversation started tentatively. The first few minutes were awkward, with Claudia trying to find a topic that might spark Luis's interest and him responding with brief answers. But as they talked, Claudia noticed Luis gradually relaxing, though he still maintained a slightly stiff posture, as if he wasn't accustomed to such encounters.

Finally, after a few attempts at small talk, Claudia decided to dive into Luis's obvious passion: technology. She asked about his work and what he loved about programming, and for the first time, Luis seemed to light up. His eyes sparkled slightly, and his tone grew more animated.

"Well, I've always been fascinated by the idea of creating something out of nothing," he said, gesturing with his hands as if trying to give shape to his thoughts. "Programming is like… building new worlds. I can take an idea in my head and turn it into something real, something functional, something people can use. It's like solving a puzzle that's always evolving."

Claudia, surprised by the passion in his voice, encouraged him to keep talking, and slowly, their conversation began to flow. Luis told her about his projects, including a task-organizing app he had started as a hobby, which was now being used by thousands of people worldwide. As he spoke, Claudia realized there was much more to Luis than she had assumed. Beneath his reserved demeanor was a curious intelligence and a desire to make the world better, even if only through lines of code.

"That sounds fascinating," Claudia said sincerely. "I've never really understood programming, but I love the idea of building something from scratch. It must be incredibly rewarding."

Luis smiled, and for the first time all evening, he seemed genuinely at ease. "It is. But it's also… lonely. I spend a lot of time in front of the screen, working alone. I guess that's why I don't go out much. Sometimes I think I should be more social, but… it's not easy."

Claudia listened intently, realizing this was the first time Luis had allowed himself to be vulnerable. She felt an unexpected connection—not in a romantic sense, but on a deeper level, understanding how hard it could be to reveal one's insecurities. She decided to open up as well.

"I get it. I'm not great at stepping out of my comfort zone either," she admitted. "That's part of why I'm doing this. It's… a personal challenge. I've always been afraid of not finding the right person, and I thought if I didn't give myself the chance to meet new people, I'd never know."

Luis nodded slowly, his expression empathetic.

"That makes sense. I think sometimes we hide behind what we know because it feels safer. But what you're doing… it's brave, Claudia. I don't know if I could do something like this."

After that shared moment of vulnerability, the atmosphere shifted. Luis began asking her questions about her life, her work, and her hobbies, and Claudia noticed she no longer had to work so hard to keep the conversation going. Luis had opened up, and while he remained reserved, he seemed to genuinely enjoy their time together.

When they finished their drinks, Luis suggested taking a short walk through the city. It was an unexpected proposal, but Claudia agreed, curious to see how the evening might unfold outside the comfort of the café. They bundled up and stepped into the chilly night. The Christmas lights bathed the streets in a warm glow, and small snowflakes began to fall, adding a magical touch to the city.

They wandered aimlessly, enjoying the shared silence and the festive decorations. Luis seemed more at ease than ever, and they eventually stopped in a nearby park where a group of children played around a small, illuminated Christmas tree.

"I've always loved Christmas," Luis said suddenly, breaking the silence. "When I was a kid, my mom and I would decorate the tree together. It was the best time of the year for me. I guess it's the only time I let myself feel a little... nostalgic."

Claudia smiled, feeling a surprising tenderness toward him.

"I used to do the same with my mom," she said. "We still do, actually. For me, Christmas is all about remembering what really matters."

Luis nodded, and for the first time, it seemed he let go of the protective shield he'd been carrying all evening.

"Maybe... we should try to remember that more often, not just at Christmas," he murmured, gazing thoughtfully at the twinkling lights.

When the clock struck nine, Claudia and Luis slowly made their way back to the city center. They had shared more than a date; they had connected in a way she hadn't anticipated. There hadn't been the spark Claudia hoped to find, but there was something equally valuable: a sense of authenticity, of having shared a genuine moment with another person.

As they reached the spot where they were to part ways, Luis hesitated, as if reluctant to end the evening. Finally, he offered her a shy smile and extended his hand, a gesture

Claudia found more meaningful than anything else.

"Thank you for tonight, Claudia. It was... different from what I expected. In a good way," he said, his eyes sincere.

"Thank you, Luis. I'm glad I got to know you better. Truly," she replied with a warm smile.

Luis nodded, gave one last glance at the glowing Christmas lights, and walked away, his steps slow and steady as snowflakes fell gently around him. Claudia stood for a moment, watching him go, marveling at how a date she had expected to be awkward had turned into one of the most sincere and meaningful experiences so far.

Back home, Claudia lit a few candles on her coffee table and sat down to write in her journal. She described the evening with a raw honesty that surprised her. There had been no romance, no spark, but there had been something else, something she couldn't quite define. Luis was a good person, someone she could imagine having a wonderful friendship with, but he wasn't the love she was searching for. Even so, the date had reminded her of something important: we all, at some point, hide behind masks of safety that prevent us from showing who we really are.

Claudia felt grateful for the evening—for the lesson learned and the realization that, even though she hadn't found the love of her life, she had met someone who reminded her of the importance of authenticity.

Before going to bed, she checked her planner: December 8th – Carlos, the adventurous traveler. Claudia smiled, knowing that each date brought her closer to the person she was meant to find, even if she didn't yet know who that would be. She turned off the lights, letting the warmth of the candles fill the room, and closed her eyes, hoping that the next night would be just as honest and meaningful as the one she had just experienced.

December 8th

The sound of the wind against the windows woke Claudia on the morning of December 8th. She stayed in bed for a few moments, listening to the gentle rain falling over the city and letting the morning's dampness slowly embrace her. Last night's date with Luis had been surprisingly sincere, but it had confirmed what she already suspected: she still hadn't found the spark she was searching for. Even so, she was grateful for the honesty and the connection they had shared, even if it wasn't romantic.

As she brewed her morning coffee, her thoughts drifted to tonight's date. Carlos, her next companion, was an avid traveler and photographer she had met a few months earlier at an art fair. They had exchanged a few words about their respective passions—his photography and her love of art exhibitions—and Claudia clearly remembered the carefree energy Carlos exuded. She knew this date would be entirely different from the previous ones. Carlos was a free spirit, someone untethered to places or routines. That intrigued her, but it also scared her a little.

The day flew by at the office, consumed by meetings and calls that dragged on longer than necessary. Laura, her inseparable work friend, joined her at lunch and asked about her expectations for the evening's date.

"So, tonight's the traveler?" Laura asked, smiling as she toyed with her fork.

"Yeah, Carlos. He's a photographer and spends most of the year traveling. He said he'd be in Madrid this week between trips, so I figured it was the perfect time to meet. I'm not sure what to expect... I have a feeling it's going to be different," Claudia replied, smiling as she stirred her salad.

"Different sounds good! I think you could use a bit of fresh air after your other dates. Maybe he'll take you somewhere exciting or share fascinating stories about his adventures," Laura suggested optimistically.

Claudia smiled, though part of her worried Carlos might be too adventurous—someone who could never settle down. Still, she decided to keep an open mind. After all, Christmas was the season for surprises.

When Claudia left the office that afternoon, the rain had stopped, but gray clouds still hung low in the sky. She walked to *La Posada del Café*, savoring the fresh air left by the storm and the earthy aroma of the rain-soaked streets. As she entered the café, Miguel greeted her with his usual warm smile, though there was a spark of curiosity in his eyes this time.

"Ready for tonight's date, Claudia?" he asked, setting a berry infusion on the counter for her.

"Yes, though I have to admit I don't know what to expect from Carlos. He's a traveler, a free spirit... I think this date will be an adventure in itself," she replied with a soft laugh.

Miguel nodded and set her drink on the table, retreating discreetly as Claudia settled in. She had arrived a few minutes early and passed the time scrolling through her phone, taking in the café's festive decorations. The twinkling lights created a cozy atmosphere, and for a moment, she allowed herself to dream about finding someone who shared her appreciation for life's small joys.

At six o'clock sharp, the door jingled softly, and Carlos walked in with an energetic stride. He wore a weathered brown leather jacket, a colorful scarf, and a backpack slung over one shoulder. His face radiated vitality, and his broad smile seemed to light up the gloomy evening. Spotting Claudia, he raised a hand in a cheerful wave.

"Claudia! Great to see you," he said, giving her a hug as natural as one between old friends reconnecting.

"Hi, Carlos. I'm glad you could make it," she replied, caught up in his good mood.

Carlos ordered an Americano, and before Claudia could say much, he launched into a story about his recent trip to Iceland. The conversation was lively from the start, and Claudia immediately felt the infectious energy Carlos brought with him. He had a way of speaking that made everything sound thrilling, from an Arctic sunset to a stroll through an Asian street market.

Carlos was a natural storyteller. Every time he spoke, it felt like he was painting vivid pictures in the air, describing remote places, exotic cultures, and fascinating people he had encountered on his travels. Claudia found herself lost in his tales, laughing at his anecdotes about nights under the stars in the Sahara Desert and marveling at the adventures he had experienced in places she could hardly imagine.

"Traveling makes me feel alive," Carlos said at one point, stirring his coffee with a spoon. "It's the only way I know to truly connect with the world. I think everyone should step out of their comfort zone at least once in their life. Seeing how other people live, experiencing other cultures... it changes your perspective on everything."

Claudia listened, captivated, but she couldn't ignore the slight knot forming in her stomach. Carlos spoke with such passion that it sometimes seemed his life was destined to be an endless series of adventures. She, on the other hand, had always dreamed of traveling but also longed for a sense of stability—to build something lasting in one place.

"It must be incredible to live that way, always on the move," she said, trying to keep the enthusiasm in her voice. "But... doesn't it get hard to be away from home all the time? Don't you miss having a place to come back to?"

Carlos smiled, but his expression turned more serious, almost wistful.

"Yeah, sometimes it is hard. There are moments when I wish I could stay put, build something with someone... but then I think about the next adventure, the next destination, and I just can't help but keep going. I guess it's just who I am," he said, shrugging with a resigned smile.

Claudia felt a mix of admiration and sadness. She knew that, while the conversation was stimulating and Carlos was a fascinating person, they probably weren't compatible in terms of what they each wanted from life.

As the evening grew colder and the plaza began to empty, Claudia and Carlos slowly made their way to the metro. Neither seemed eager to end the date, but both understood the night was coming to a close. They said goodbye at the metro entrance, standing under the warm glow of a streetlamp.

"This was an incredible night, Claudia," Carlos said sincerely. "I'm glad we got to spend this time together. You're... different from most people I meet."

"So are you, Carlos. Thank you for sharing your stories with me. It's been... an adventure," Claudia replied, feeling her words fall short of expressing everything she wanted to say.

Carlos seemed to understand because he smiled and gave her a warm hug before planting a soft kiss on her cheek.

"I hope you find what you're looking for, Claudia. Don't let anyone hold you back," he said, waving one last goodbye before disappearing into the bustling metro crowd.

Claudia stood for a moment at the metro entrance, watching Carlos walk away, feeling a mix of nostalgia and relief. She knew Carlos wasn't the kind of man she could build something stable with, but she also knew this night had been meaningful. She had realized that, while she admired Carlos's freedom, she needed something more—something that wasn't fleeting like a spark in the dark.

When she got home, Claudia took off her coat and lit the Christmas tree lights. Pouring herself a glass of wine, she sank onto the couch, her mind brimming with thoughts. She had enjoyed the night, but she also felt more certain than ever about what she truly wanted in a relationship. It wasn't just the thrill of the moment or the intensity of a fleeting adventure; she needed someone who could be her partner in every sense—not just in the exciting times.

She wrote about the evening in her journal, trying to capture every detail, from Carlos's stories to the scent of roasted chestnuts in the plaza. She knew this date had been another step on her journey, one that brought her closer, little by little, to the person she was destined to find.

Turning off the lights, she let the warmth of the Christmas tree envelop her and prepared for sleep. On her calendar, the next date awaited: December 9th – Juan, the kind architect. Claudia smiled to herself, sensing that something big was about to happen—as if Christmas was saving a special surprise for her, one she couldn't yet foresee.

December 9th

On December 9th, Claudia woke up feeling a strange excitement she hadn't experienced on any of her previous dates. Her evening with Carlos had been thrilling, but it had also brought her the realization that she wanted something more stable, something deeper. Juan, her date for that night, seemed like the kind of man who could offer her that. She had met Juan through mutual friends at an art exhibition opening, and since then, they'd kept in touch occasionally, exchanging a few words at social gatherings. She'd always found him to be a calm, grounded presence—an intriguing combination.

As she prepared to head to the office, Claudia chose an outfit that balanced elegance with comfort: dark jeans, a beige turtleneck sweater, and a warm jacket. She wanted to feel good about herself without giving the impression that she'd overthought her look. Christmas was getting closer, and with it came the feeling that something special could happen at any moment.

At the office, Laura asked her about the date with Carlos, and Claudia gave her a summary of the night, sharing the fascinating stories but also pointing out that he wasn't what she was looking for.

"So, tonight's with the architect, right?" Laura asked, a curious smile on her face.

"Yes, Juan. He's... different. I don't know him well, but he seems to be someone who's grounded. I need that, Laura. Something real, something authentic," Claudia replied, feeling that for the first time, she was voicing exactly what she wanted.

"Well, I hope this date gives you exactly what you're looking for," Laura said, raising her coffee cup in a toast. "Here's to a perfect night!"

Claudia smiled, caught up in her friend's enthusiasm, and promised herself to keep an open mind. She knew there was something about Juan that had drawn her in from the start, but she didn't want to get her hopes up too quickly. Still, the thought of the date kept her in a state of anticipation all day.

When Claudia left work that afternoon, the air was colder than usual, but it didn't matter. She felt full of energy as she walked toward La Posada del Café, with Christmas lights twinkling above her like a constant reminder that the magic of the season was all around. When she arrived, Miguel greeted her with a smile that seemed to know her better than she knew herself.

"You've got a good feeling tonight, don't you?" Miguel asked as he prepared a cinnamon latte.

"I do. I don't know why, but I feel like tonight will be different," Claudia replied, trying to hide her nervous smile.

She settled into her usual table by the window, looking out at the lit street as she took small sips of her coffee. She had arrived ten minutes early, wanting to calm her nerves before the date. At six o'clock on the dot, the café door opened, and Juan stepped in, shaking off the light snow that had begun to fall. He wore a dark coat and a gray scarf, and his eyes lit up when he saw Claudia.

"Hi! I hope I'm not late," Juan said with a warm smile as he made his way to the table.

"No, right on time," Claudia responded, feeling an unexpected calm as he sat down across from her.

They ordered their drinks, and the conversation began with a smoothness that surprised Claudia. Juan had a calm way of speaking, without pretension or anxiety. He told her about his work as an architect, his recent projects, and how passionate he was about designing spaces that were not only functional but also told a story. Claudia, fascinated, asked him about his influences and found herself genuinely interested in his answers.

"I've always thought of architecture as a way of telling stories through space," Juan said at one point, gazing absentmindedly at the foam on his coffee. "The lines, the shadows, the light... everything speaks of who we are and how we want to live. Christmas is a perfect example: we transform spaces to make them cozy, to reflect how we feel during this time of year."

Claudia felt an immediate connection to his words. She, too, believed in the power of stories, and the way Juan described architecture as a form of expression struck her as incredibly attractive. It was the first time, in all her dates, that she felt someone shared her passion for details, for the essence behind things.

The conversation flowed effortlessly, and Claudia discovered they had much more in common than she had imagined. They talked about their tastes in books, music, and art, finding that they both appreciated the small things in life: a hot cup of coffee on a cold morning, the quiet of a walk at sunset, or the way Christmas lights transformed the city into a warmer, more inviting place.

Juan told her about his family, how his parents used to decorate their home at Christmas when he was a child, and how he had carried on the tradition by decorating his own apartment each year. Claudia listened, feeling a growing warmth in her chest. It was rare to find someone who shared that love for Christmas and the traditions that came with it.

"And you? Do you have any Christmas traditions that you always keep?" Juan asked, with genuine curiosity.

Claudia smiled, recalling the afternoons spent with her mother baking cookies and decorating the tree.

"I always bake gingerbread cookies with my mom. It's something we've done since I was little. There's no Christmas without those cookies at home," she replied, laughing. "It's simple, but it makes me feel at home."

Juan nodded, a soft expression on his face.

"I like that. Christmas is all about those little things, isn't it? The things that make us feel at home, even when we're far away."

There was a moment of silence between them, but it wasn't awkward. Claudia felt that, for the first time, she was on a date where she didn't have to force the conversation or search for a connection. They were just there, enjoying the moment.

After finishing their drinks, Juan suggested they take a walk. The snow was falling heavier now, covering the city with a thin white layer that shimmered under the Christmas lights. Claudia happily agreed, and together they left the café, bundling up against the cold as they walked through the streets filled with people.

They made their way to Retiro Park, one of Claudia's favorite spots in the city, and walked slowly along the snow-covered paths. The lights from the streetlamps illuminated their way, and the shadows of the trees cast whimsical shapes on the snowy ground. The air was crisp and clean, and each breath seemed to fill her with a tranquility she hadn't felt in a long time.

"I've always loved this park in winter," Claudia said quietly, as if not wanting to disturb the stillness of the moment. "It's like the snow transforms it into a completely different place."

Juan nodded, looking around with a smile.

"It's true. There's something magical about the snow, don't you think? It's like it covers up all the bad, the ugly, and only leaves what really matters," he replied, giving her a meaningful look that Claudia couldn't help but notice.

They continued walking until they reached the lake, where Christmas lights adorned the trees around the water. They stopped there, in silence, watching as the snowflakes slowly fell on the lake's surface, creating tiny circles that vanished within seconds. Claudia felt time stand still, as if that moment was perfect in its simplicity.

While they watched the lake, Juan told her a story about his most recent project: restoring an old house on the outskirts of Madrid. He talked about the details, how he wanted to preserve the original essence of the place while adding modern touches to make it more livable. Claudia listened, captivated by each word, feeling like she was getting to know a side of him that few others knew.

"You're really passionate about what you do, Juan," she said, finally, feeling she needed to say it out loud. "I like that."

Juan smiled, but there was something in his expression that showed more than simple satisfaction.

"It's easy to be passionate when you find something you really care about," he replied, looking at her with an intensity that made Claudia feel an unexpected warmth in her chest, despite the cold around them.

There was a moment of silence, one of those silences that speaks more than any words. Claudia realized she was enjoying Juan's company in a way she hadn't expected, that there was something in his presence that made her feel calm and excited at the same time. It was like she had finally found someone who saw the world the same way she did, someone who understood the importance of the little things.

Suddenly, a group of children playing in the snow near the lake ran past them, laughing and throwing snowballs. Claudia and Juan laughed too, caught up in their infectious joy, and it was in that moment that Juan did something unexpected: he gently took Claudia's hand, intertwining his fingers with hers.

Claudia felt a small jolt, but she didn't pull her hand away. On the contrary, she felt a warmth spread through her, a sense of familiarity and comfort she hadn't experienced in any of her previous dates. She looked at Juan and saw in his eyes the same mixture of joy and calm she felt.

When the clock struck nine, and the snow began to fall more heavily, they decided to head back. Juan walked her to the door of her apartment, and Claudia didn't want the night to end. They had talked about so many things, but she still felt there was much more to discover. They stopped at the entrance, still holding hands, and both smiled at the same time.

"Thank you for tonight, Claudia. It's been... perfect," Juan said, with a sincerity that left no room for doubt.

"Thank you, Juan. It's been one of the best nights I've had in a long time," she replied, feeling that she wasn't exaggerating in the slightest.

There was a moment when both of them hesitated, when the possibility of a kiss seemed to hang in the air between them. But in the end, they said goodbye with a long, warm embrace that felt like a promise of more encounters in the future.

"We'll see each other soon, right?" Juan asked, before pulling away, a hopeful smile on his face.

"Definitely," Claudia replied, feeling something inside her light up with the certainty that this wouldn't be the last time she saw him.

She stood at the entrance to her apartment until Juan's figure disappeared into the distance, and only then did she go upstairs, overwhelmed by a calm sense of happiness.

When Claudia arrived home, she couldn't help but smile at the sight of her Christmas tree, its lights softly twinkling in the darkness of the living room. She knew that tonight had been different, that something inside her had changed. It wasn't just the conversation or their shared interests; there was a real connection, something she hadn't felt with any of her previous dates.

She poured herself a glass of wine and sat on the couch, gazing at the tree as she reflected on the evening. She had found someone she could truly be herself with, someone who shared her perspective on the world and, at the same time, challenged her to see things in a new way. She wrote in her journal about the date, detailing each moment, every word exchanged with Juan, each sensation she had experienced under the falling snow.

For the first time in a long time, Claudia felt genuinely hopeful about the possibility of finding love before Christmas. Maybe, just maybe, Juan was the man she had been searching for without even realizing it.

She turned off the lights, let the calm of the night wrap around her, and snuggled under the blankets, her mind full of warm memories and unspoken promises. There were still dates ahead, but she knew that something had shifted on her journey that night. Christmas was near, and the magic of the unexpected still enveloped her like a cloak of light.

December 10th

Claudia woke up on December 10th with her mind flooded with thoughts of Juan. The date with him had been perfect, different from all the others. Since they had said goodbye at the door of La Posada del Café, Claudia hadn't been able to stop thinking about his genuine smile, how effortlessly the conversation had flowed, and the unspoken promise of seeing each other again. However, she also knew that her holiday challenge was far from over. She had decided to continue with the dates, even though part of her felt guilty about meeting other men after what she had felt with Juan.

As she got ready for work, she carefully chose her outfit: a white wool sweater, dark pants, and a gray cashmere scarf. She wanted to look professional and be prepared for the date she had scheduled for that afternoon, but in her mind, everything kept comparing itself to Juan. The Christmas lights decorating the street, the smell of roasted chestnuts in the air—everything reminded her of that magical evening. She tried to convince herself that this was all part of the process, that she needed to stick to the schedule to be sure of her feelings.

She arrived at the office early and tried to focus on her work. Yet, her thoughts kept drifting back to the night of December 9th, to the way Juan had looked at her, and to how that gaze had made her feel. Laura, her friend and colleague, immediately noticed.

"Okay, tell me everything. I know you too well to not notice that something important is on your mind," said Laura, setting a coffee on Claudia's desk.

Claudia smiled, feeling exposed, and took a sip of her coffee before answering.

"I met someone... different," she confessed, feeling that saying it out loud made everything more real. "His name is Juan, he's an architect, and I think it was the most perfect date I've had in a long time."

Laura looked at her with a mix of surprise and excitement.

"So, what are you doing here, so calm, and not on a second date with him?" she asked, laughing.

"Because I'm not done with the calendar yet. I want to keep going with the dates, at least until I'm sure of what I feel. I don't want to let the excitement of one night throw me off the plan I made," Claudia replied, though doubt crept into her words.

Laura sighed but nodded, understanding her friend's reasons.

"Well, you better prepare for whatever comes next. But if Juan is as special as you say, I don't think your decision to stick to the calendar will last long," she said, winking.

The rest of the day passed slowly, as if the hours in the office had come to a standstill. Claudia reviewed contracts, took calls, and answered emails, but her mind kept returning to Juan. At 5:30, she left the office and headed to La Posada del Café, the café that had become her haven in this search for love.

At six on the dot, Iván walked into the cafe. He was a tall, attractive man with impeccable style and an air of confidence that Claudia immediately recognized. He wore a stylish black coat and a red scarf, moving with the assurance of someone who knew they were being noticed. Claudia smiled as he approached, though something inside her told her that something didn't quite fit.

"Hi, Claudia, nice to meet you," Iván said, giving her two kisses on the cheeks before sitting down in front of her with a smooth motion.

"Hi, Iván, thanks for coming," she replied, trying to sound enthusiastic.

The conversation started off superficial, talking about their jobs, hobbies, and plans for the holidays. Iván seemed more interested in impressing her than in getting to know her, as much of the conversation centered around his sports car, personal achievements, and luxury trips. Claudia listened, but she couldn't help comparing every word with the date she had had with Juan. She felt that the warmth and sincerity she had experienced the night before were completely absent from this conversation.

"So, what car do you drive?" Iván asked at one point, genuinely curious if Claudia shared his passion for cars.

Claudia smiled, a little uncomfortable.

"Well, it's nothing fancy. I drive a small car, something practical for the city. I've never really been into cars, to be honest," she responded, sensing the disappointment on Iván's face.

The rest of the date continued in the same manner. Iván spoke enthusiastically, but everything he said felt superficial, as if he was trying to impress rather than connect. When the date ended, Claudia felt a mix of relief and frustration. She knew Iván wasn't what she was looking for, but she also knew that part of her disappointment came from the inevitable comparison with Juan.

They said goodbye with a cordial handshake, and Claudia left the café feeling the cold of the night wrapping around her. She walked slowly toward her apartment, reflecting on what this date had made clear to her: the connection she had felt with Juan was not something she could ignore. Still, she felt torn between her commitment to the calendar and her desire to take a chance on something that had surprised her.

When she arrived at her apartment, Claudia turned on the Christmas tree lights, which blinked softly in the dim light. She took off her coat, made herself a hot infusion, and sat down on the couch, her legs crossed under a blanket. She gazed out the window at the city lights and allowed herself to reflect on everything that had happened since she began this challenge.

The dating calendar had started as a way to challenge herself, to step out of her comfort zone and find something that had eluded her for years. She had met interesting men, but none of them had left a mark on her heart. Until Juan came along. There was something about him that made her feel alive, that made her believe finding love before Christmas was possible. Yet, she resisted abandoning her plan for the sake of just one date.

The sound of her phone pulled her from her thoughts. It was a message from Juan:

"Hi, Claudia. I hope you had a good day. I haven't been able to stop thinking about our date. I'd love to see you again. How about a walk?"

Claudia's heart skipped a beat as she read the message. What she had feared was happening: Juan was still present in her mind, in her thoughts, and now, in her desires. She took a deep breath before replying, knowing that any decision she made would impact what she was looking for.

"Hi, Juan. I'd love to. I need some time to think about what I really want. See you soon."

She sent the message before her doubts could stop her, feeling a mix of excitement and relief as the notification disappeared. She wanted to accept the invitation, but she also knew that the final decision had not yet been made.

As the night wore on, Claudia decided that, at least until she completed the Advent calendar, she would continue with the dates she had planned. She knew she wanted to see Juan again, but she also knew she needed to make sure that what she felt wasn't just the result of the moment's excitement. If, after all the dates, she still thought of him, then she would know it was something more.

She turned off the living room lights and lay down in bed, watching the reflection of the Christmas lights through the window. Her thoughts were a tangled mess of emotions, expectations, and fears, but also of hope. Christmas was approaching quickly, and Claudia knew that soon she would have to make a decision that would change her life.

She closed her eyes, letting the fatigue of the day surround her, and fell asleep with a feeling of uncertainty and joy. She knew that, one way or another, the challenge she had started on December 1st was nearing a turning point, and that what she felt in the next few dates would define what came next.

The magic of Christmas hadn't ended yet, and Claudia, though confused, felt that something wonderful was about to happen.

December 11th

December 11th began with a sense of emptiness for Claudia. She woke up with her mind still lingering on the date from the previous night with Iván, the man who, although attractive, had proven to be superficial and incapable of connecting with her in an authentic way. Claudia had decided to continue with her dating schedule, but she was feeling increasingly emotionally drained. She realized that, although she had met some interesting men, none had reached her heart the way Juan had. And yet, here she was, ready to face another date.

She got up slowly, feeling the cold of the floor beneath her bare feet as she walked to the kitchen. She made herself a strong cup of coffee, hoping the warmth of the drink would give her the energy to face the day. She still hadn't replied to Juan's message, where he suggested a walk for the weekend. The pressure to keep going with the dates while her thoughts kept returning to him made her feel trapped in her own challenge.

Sitting by the window, Claudia watched the snow gently fall over the streets of Madrid, covering everything with a white layer that seemed to erase any imperfections. In a way, she wished it were that easy for her to erase her doubts. Tonight's date was with Marcos, a high-powered executive working in the corporate world. She knew his type well: always busy men, with schedules so tight that any interaction turned into a business matter. She didn't have high expectations, but she had decided to give him a chance.

"Maybe I'm being too picky," Claudia thought as she took a sip of her hot coffee. But deep down, she knew it wasn't about being picky—it was about staying true to what she really wanted. She had to go through with tonight's date, even though a part of her was starting to wonder if it was really worth it.

The day at the office was monotonous and overwhelming. Claudia tried to focus on her cases, drafting legal documents and responding to the emails piling up in her inbox. But her mind kept drifting back to tonight's date, and to the unanswered message from Juan. Every time she thought of him, she felt a warmth in her chest, a memory of the shared laughter and the comfort of his presence.

Laura, noticing Claudia was distracted, came over to her desk with a concerned smile.

"Come on, what's going on now?" she asked, leaning against the edge of Claudia's desk. "Yesterday you told me Iván wasn't what you expected, but today it looks like you've got something else on your mind. Is it tonight's date?"

Claudia sighed, resting her chin on her palm.

"Yes… I have a date with Marcos, an executive who seems to live for his work. I'm not expecting much, to be honest. And I can't stop thinking about Juan. Every time I meet someone, I compare them to him, and it's driving me crazy," she confessed, feeling that talking to Laura was helping her sort through her thoughts.

Laura looked at her with a mix of empathy and disapproval.

"I'm not surprised, Claudia. If you already know what you want, why keep going with this? I understand you took on this challenge, but I don't think you should continue if your heart has already made a decision," she said, with her usual straightforward tone.

Claudia nodded, knowing Laura was right. But part of her still felt she needed to fulfill the commitment she had made. It was hard to leave something unfinished, especially when she had put so much effort into this search.

"Maybe tonight will give me the clarity I need," she finally said, trying to convince herself.

At six o'clock, Claudia arrived at La Posada del Café, as usual. The café was busier than usual, with people seeking refuge from the cold outside, enjoying the warm and festive atmosphere. Christmas lights flickered gently over the windows, and the aroma of cinnamon and hot chocolate filled the air. Claudia took off her coat, shook the snow from her boots, and sat at her usual table, waiting for Marcos to arrive.

By 6:20, Claudia was starting to feel uneasy. She looked at the clock for the third time and wondered if Marcos had forgotten about the date. At 6:30, he finally walked through the door, phone in hand, frowning. He wore a sharp dark gray suit and an elegant scarf, but there was a stiffness in his face that Claudia noticed immediately.

"Sorry I'm late, Claudia," he said, quickly kissing her on the cheek and sitting down hastily. "The meeting at the office ran longer than I expected. You know how it is, always something that needs to be sorted."

Claudia smiled politely, though she already felt a slight sense of discouragement. Marcos placed his phone on the table, but it wasn't long before he picked it up again to respond to a message. They ordered coffee, and Claudia tried to start a conversation about their work and interests, but every answer from Marcos was brief and rushed, as if his mind was elsewhere.

"So, how do you celebrate Christmas?" Claudia asked, trying to lighten the mood.

Marcos shrugged, glancing at his phone.

"Oh, well, my family's never been very traditional. I usually travel for work at this time, but this year I decided to stay. Maybe I'll have dinner with my parents, but it's not a big deal," he answered, distracted.

Claudia tried to keep the conversation going, but every question she asked seemed to fall flat. After half an hour, Marcos was already checking his watch, clearly impatient. Claudia was feeling more and more uncomfortable, aware that this date was pointless.

Finally, Marcos put his half-empty coffee cup back on the table and shot Claudia a quick look.

"I'm sorry, but I have another meeting in twenty minutes. It's been a pleasure meeting you, Claudia. I hope we have the chance to talk more sometime," he said, standing up and grabbing his coat in one swift motion.

Claudia felt a mix of disbelief and relief at the same time. She said her polite goodbyes, knowing that there was no real intention to see each other again. Marcos left the café, already talking on his phone, and Claudia sat alone at the table, watching him walk away without looking back.

Claudia took a sip of her now-cold coffee and stared out the window. There was something almost liberating in this disappointment, something that pushed her to make a decision she had been avoiding for days. She pulled out her phone and began reviewing the calendar she had created for the dates, scrolling through the names of the men still scheduled for the coming days. She felt a sudden calm as she looked at them, and then made a decision.

She deleted each of the upcoming dates, removing the notifications from her phone one by one. When she finished, she left the phone on the table and felt a weight lift off her shoulders. She knew her search wasn't over, but she also knew she didn't need more dates to know what she wanted. What she was looking for wasn't in a series of scheduled meetings, but in the authentic connection she had felt with Juan.

She left money on the table to cover the coffee and walked out of the café, leaving behind the routine of dates that had filled her days since December 1st. The snow continued to fall gently over the city, and Claudia walked slowly down the illuminated streets, feeling that with every step, she was getting closer to the real decision she had to make.

That night, when she arrived at her apartment, Claudia turned on the Christmas tree lights and sat on the couch, surrounded by the warmth of home. She took out her phone and saw a message from Juan, wishing her goodnight. She stared at the screen, feeling the urgency to be honest, to tell him what she truly felt.

She wrote him a long message, telling him how she felt. She put the phone aside and snuggled into the couch, watching the tree lights flicker in the dark.

For the first time in weeks, Claudia felt like she was following her heart, and though she didn't know what would come next, she was sure she had taken the right step. Christmas was fast approaching, and though the dating calendar had come to an end, her real story was just beginning.

December 12th

On December 12th, Claudia woke up with a different feeling than in previous days. She had decided to cancel most of the remaining dates on her schedule, but there was still one left: Hugo. Although the decision to focus on what she truly wanted was nearly made, she felt she owed it to herself to give this last encounter a chance to confirm that she was making the right choice.

Since leaving behind the disappointing date with Marcos, her mind had been consumed by thoughts of Juan. Her days at the office passed quickly, but in her free moments, her thoughts always returned to the easy conversation and the genuine connection she'd felt with him. However, Hugo was a man with good references: kind, charming, and highly recommended by a mutual friend. She thought that if this date didn't work out, then her search would be over, because her intuition told her that Juan was the right person.

She got out of bed and prepared a light breakfast, trying to calm her nerves. She dressed in a dark green sweater that accentuated the color of her eyes and a pair of fitted jeans. She wanted to feel comfortable, but also ready for whatever came next. As she looked at herself in the hallway mirror before leaving, adjusting a rebellious strand of hair, she reminded herself that this was the last date—the final effort before leaving behind the advent calendar she'd designed for her love life.

Claudia arrived at *La Posada del Café* at six o'clock, as usual. The place was busier than usual, with people seeking respite from the winter chill, its warm lights and Christmas decorations creating a magical atmosphere. It had snowed lightly that morning, and the wet footprints of earlier customers marked the entrance floor. She greeted Miguel, the waiter who knew her preferences well and had become a silent accomplice to her dates. This time, however, there was something different in the way he smiled at her, as if he knew this date was the last of a series he had closely observed.

She sat at the table by the window, the same one she'd shared with every man she had met since starting her challenge. Snow continued to fall gently outside, and as Claudia waited for Hugo, she realized something inside her had changed. She had begun this search with the hope of finding love before Christmas, but now she felt that what she really wanted wasn't to fill that void with just anyone, but with someone who made her feel alive and understood. And although she still had to meet Hugo, deep down she already felt that person was Juan.

At 6:05, Hugo arrived. He was a tall man with brown hair and clear eyes, carrying a friendly smile that conveyed confidence from the very first moment. He wore a long dark gray coat and a blue sweater underneath. As he entered, he took off his wool hat and headed straight for Claudia, smiling warmly.

"Hi, Claudia! Sorry for the slight delay, I was dealing with the Christmas traffic," he said, giving her two quick kisses on the cheek before sitting down.

"No worries, Hugo. The traffic at this time of year is crazy," Claudia replied with a kind smile.

They ordered two coffees and started chatting. From the beginning, the conversation flowed pleasantly. Hugo was charming, kind, and knew how to keep the conversation interesting. They talked about their jobs, their families, and their childhood Christmas memories. Claudia realized there were many things she liked about him, but something was still missing. She didn't feel that spark, that excitement she had felt when she was with Juan. He was pleasant, but not thrilling, and as the minutes passed, she realized that this date wasn't going to change what she had already decided deep down.

As the conversation went on, Claudia tried to delve into some topics that were important to her. She spoke about her dreams, what she expected from a relationship, and what Christmas meant to her—sharing it with someone special. Hugo responded with the same kindness he'd shown from the start, but every answer seemed to stay on the surface. There was no desire to dig deeper, to understand what she truly meant. It was as though they were talking on different levels, without the depth that Claudia had been searching for.

"Christmas has always been an important time for me," Claudia said at one point, trying to steer the conversation into more intimate territory. "It's a time to reconnect with family, to enjoy each other's company, and to find the magic in the simple things."

Hugo smiled, but his response was predictable.

"Yeah, it's a nice time of year, though sometimes I think it's all too commercial. But I get what you mean, I like seeing the lights and Christmas markets, although I don't put too much importance on all that. In the end, I think the most important thing is being comfortable, right?"

Claudia nodded, though she knew that wasn't really what she wanted to hear. To her, Christmas was more than that—a time to make memories, to open up her heart, and to share. And while Hugo seemed like a wonderful man in many ways, he wasn't the person she was looking for.

As the date neared its end, Claudia felt a decision form clearly in her mind. She had reached the end of her personal challenge, and now she knew it was time to put the dates behind her and focus on what she truly wanted. Hugo was charming, kind, and polite, but he lacked the emotional depth she needed. The conversation had been pleasant, but without passion, without that spark Claudia had felt with Juan.

When they finished their coffees, Hugo suggested going for a walk through the illuminated streets of Madrid, but Claudia gently declined the offer.

"It's been a very nice afternoon, Hugo. But I think I need some time to think," she said, trying to be honest without hurting his feelings.

Hugo took it gracefully, smiling understandingly and giving her a kiss on the cheek before saying goodbye.

"I understand, Claudia. It's been a pleasure meeting you, and I hope you find what you're looking for," he said, without a trace of resentment.

When he left, Claudia sat alone at the table for a few minutes, staring at the Christmas lights reflected in the window. She knew she had made the right decision. She left the café, bundling up against the cold, and began walking aimlessly through the streets of Madrid. It had snowed during the date, and the city was covered in a thin layer of sparkling snow that crunched beneath her boots.

On her way home, Claudia felt as if a weight had been lifted from her shoulders. For the first time in weeks, she had no more dates scheduled, no commitments or expectations to fulfill. She only had the certainty that she needed to follow her heart, knowing that what she was really searching for couldn't be found in a series of arranged dates.

When she got home, she turned on the Christmas tree lights and sat on the couch, watching the shadows cast by the ornaments on the wall. She knew what she had to do.

Claudia closed her eyes, feeling a joy that filled her entire being. She had finished her advent calendar, but the most important thing was that she had found what she was truly looking for. Her heart had chosen, and the magic of Christmas surrounded her, promising that the best was yet to come.

December 13th

December 13th dawned with a special kind of silence in Madrid. The snow that had fallen overnight covered the city like a white blanket, as if time had stopped. Claudia woke up early, nestled under her blankets, feeling a sense of peace and anticipation she hadn't remembered experiencing before. She had left behind her "advent calendar" challenge of romantic dates, and with it, the appointments that had filled each day since the beginning of December. Now, she found herself at a crossroads: she needed to decide what she truly wanted.

She got up slowly, put on her robe, and made her way to the kitchen to prepare a cup of coffee. She turned on the Christmas tree lights and sat on the couch, letting the warmth of the drink soothe her hands as she gazed at the twinkling lights. She couldn't stop thinking about Juan, the connection they had shared during their date, and how, even though she had met other men since then, no one had made her feel the way he had.

The decision to cancel her remaining dates had been freeing, but also terrifying. Claudia knew that taking a risk with Juan meant opening her heart and exposing herself to the possibility that things wouldn't turn out as she hoped. But something deep inside her told her that it was worth trying.

She decided that she needed a change of scenery to clear her thoughts, so she bundled up, put on her favorite scarf, and went for a walk through the snow-covered streets of Madrid. The cold, fresh air woke her up completely, and as her boots crunched through the snow, she felt more certain about what she needed to do.

Without realizing it, her steps led her to La Posada del Café, the place where it had all started. She entered, greeted by the cozy warmth and the scent of cinnamon and coffee that filled the air. Miguel, the waiter, smiled as he saw her.

"Claudia! What a surprise to see you here at this hour. The usual coffee?" he asked while wiping down the counter.

Claudia nodded, grateful for the familiarity of the place. She sat at her usual spot by the window and watched as the Christmas lights lit up the exterior. This corner had become a refuge for her, a place where she had met all the men from her advent calendar, but also where she had met Juan.

When Miguel brought her coffee, she thanked him and settled into her thoughts. Her phone lay on the table, and although she didn't want to check it, she couldn't ignore the urge to send Juan a message. It had been a few days since their last conversation, and although he had said he was willing to wait for her, Claudia knew she couldn't let more time pass.

As she stirred her coffee with the spoon, something important occurred to her: she didn't need more dates, more analysis, or more doubts. She knew what she wanted, and what she wanted was to be with Juan.

Her heart pounding, Claudia took her phone and opened the conversation with Juan. For a moment, she stared at the blank screen, wondering how to express what she felt without seeming insecure or impulsive. Finally, she let her emotions guide her fingers.

"Hi, Juan. I've been thinking a lot about us since our date, and I feel there's something special between us that I don't want to ignore. I know I said I needed time to sort out my feelings, but I think I know now: I want to take a chance with you. Can we meet tonight?"

She pressed send before fear could stop her and left the phone on the table, feeling her heart racing. Now, all she could do was wait.

As she sipped her coffee, she tried to distract herself by watching the people coming and going in the café. Some were alone, lost in their own thoughts, while others arrived in pairs or small groups, laughing and chatting with the Christmas spirit in the air. Claudia couldn't help but imagine what it would be like to spend Christmas with Juan, sharing moments like these and creating memories together.

Her phone vibrated, pulling her from her thoughts. She picked it up nervously and saw Juan's reply.

"Hi, Claudia. You have no idea how happy it makes me to receive this message. Of course, I want to see you. How about 6 p.m. at our café?"

Claudia smiled, feeling a wave of relief and excitement wash over her. She quickly replied, confirming the date, and realized that the day of reflection she had planned was turning into something much more thrilling.

On her way home, Claudia took her time getting ready. Even though it wasn't a formal date, she wanted to look good. She chose a simple but elegant burgundy dress, paired with a gray wool scarf and a long coat. As she prepared in front of the mirror, she tried to calm her nerves, reminding herself that this was just a conversation with someone she trusted, someone who had already shown he cared for her.

When the clock struck 5:30, Claudia left her apartment and walked toward La Posada del Café. The snow had stopped, but the air was still cold and crisp, making the Christmas lights along the streets seem even brighter. As she approached the café, her heart beat faster. She knew tonight would be important, that it would mark the beginning of something new.

Juan was already at the café when Claudia arrived. He was sitting at the table by the window, a cup of coffee in front of him, looking out onto the street as if waiting for her. When he saw her enter, his face lit up with a warm smile that made Claudia feel at home.

"Hi, Claudia," he said, standing up to greet her.

"Hi, Juan. Sorry to keep you waiting," she replied, returning his smile as she sat down across from him.

The atmosphere between them was calm, yet full of anticipation. After ordering coffee, Claudia took a deep breath and decided to be honest.

"Juan, I wanted to see you because I feel there's something important between us. Since our first date, I haven't stopped thinking about you. I've spent the last few days trying to convince myself that I should stick to my plan, but I've realized that I don't need more dates to know what I want. And what I want is to give us a chance, to give this a chance," she said, her voice full of emotion.

Juan listened intently, his eyes reflecting a mix of surprise and joy. When she finished, he reached across the table and gently held her hand.

"Claudia, you don't know how much it means to me to hear that. Since I met you, I knew there was something special about you, something I wanted to discover. It makes me so happy to know that you feel the same. I want to be with you, I want to build something real, and I'm willing to take the risk with you," he replied, his sincerity making Claudia feel that everything was worth it.

After talking for a while longer, they decided to go for a walk. The streets were quiet, with few people strolling under the Christmas lights, and the cold air made the warmth of their intertwined hands even more comforting.

They walked aimlessly, talking about everything and nothing, sharing Christmas memories and dreams for the future. Claudia felt that every word they shared brought her closer to him, and that each step they took together was a reminder that she had made the right decision.

Finally, they reached a small square where a massive Christmas tree adorned with lights stood at the center. They stopped in front of the tree, admiring its beauty, and Juan turned to Claudia with a serious but tender expression.

"Claudia, this Christmas is different from any other I've experienced. And it's because you're here. I don't know what the future holds for us, but I want you to know that I'm here, with you, for whatever comes," he said, looking her in the eyes.

Claudia felt her eyes fill with tears, but this time they were tears of happiness.

"I'm here too, Juan. And I want to be with you because I know what we have is special," she replied, before he hugged her under the lights of the tree.

The snow began to fall again as they embraced, as if the whole world was celebrating their decision to begin something together. In that moment, Claudia knew she had found what she was looking for, and that this Christmas would be the most special of all.

December 14th

December 14th dawned with a special kind of energy for Claudia. The excitement of her decision the night before and the warm reunion with Juan had filled her heart with hope and anticipation. Although she had spent many Christmases with her family, facing the same old questions about her relationship status, this time she felt something had changed. She had chosen to follow her heart, and now, more than ever, she was sure she had made the right choice.

She woke up early, made her coffee, and reviewed her to-do list at work. The day passed quickly with contracts to review and calls to attend to, but Claudia had a sparkle in her eyes. By four in the afternoon, she closed her laptop, gathered her things, and left the office, her heart beating fast for the date she had scheduled with Juan that evening.

They had agreed to meet at six at the city's Christmas market, a magical place filled with lights, decorations, and small stalls selling everything from traditional sweets to handmade crafts. Claudia couldn't think of a better place to spend another evening with him.

Before leaving home, she took her time getting ready. She chose a camel-colored wool coat, a simple black dress, and comfortable boots. She wrapped herself in a red scarf that matched her lipstick, and as she looked at herself in the mirror, she smiled. She felt excited, as if she was about to experience a moment she would remember forever.

The Christmas market was a spectacle of lights and colors when Claudia arrived. The streets were full of families, couples, and groups of friends strolling between the stalls, enjoying the festive atmosphere. Lights hung from side to side, creating a glowing sky, and the air was filled with the scent of hot chocolate, freshly baked cookies, and roasted chestnuts.

Claudia walked through the crowd, looking for Juan, and it didn't take long to find him. He was waiting by a stall selling Christmas ornaments, dressed in a dark grey coat and a black scarf that made him look more attractive than ever. When he saw her, his face lit up with a smile that made Claudia forget the cold of the night.

"Hello, Claudia," he said, walking up to greet her with a kiss on the cheek. "You look stunning."

"Hi, Juan. You too. This place is incredible, don't you think?" she replied, feeling her heart race with his proximity.

"Yeah, but I'm even happier that you're here. Come on, I want to show you something," Juan said, taking her hand naturally.

Claudia felt the warmth of his hand in hers and let him guide her through the market, enjoying the bustle and the joy surrounding them.

They walked between the stalls, stopping every now and then to admire the products or try some Christmas treats. At one of the stalls, Juan bought two cups of hot chocolate and handed one to Claudia as they continued strolling. The steam rose from the cups, and the warmth of the drink contrasted with the cold of the night.

"Did you know this market has been around for over a hundred years?" Juan asked, taking a sip of his chocolate.

"No idea. It's amazing to think about how many people have passed through here over the years, enjoying Christmas," Claudia replied, looking around.

"I've always thought there's something magical about places like this. It's as if time stops for a moment, and all that matters is the present," he said, looking her straight in the eyes.

Claudia felt her cheeks flush, and not just because of the cold. There was something in the way Juan spoke, in the way he looked at her, that made her feel like she was exactly where she was meant to be.

They continued exploring, laughing together, and trying delights like nougat and marzipan. At a stall selling handmade ornaments, Claudia stopped to admire a wooden star carved with delicate details.

"It's beautiful," she said, holding it between her hands.

"It suits you," Juan commented, smiling as he watched her. "I think you should have it."

Before Claudia could respond, he had already paid the vendor and was handing her the star with a smile.

"It's a gift. So you'll remember this night," he said.

Claudia took the star, moved by the gesture, and felt a warmth spreading through her chest.

As they continued walking, they arrived at a central square where a giant Christmas tree was lit up with hundreds of lights. Around it, couples and families were taking photos, while a choir sang carols, filling the air with joy.

"It's beautiful," Claudia said, gazing at the tree in admiration.

"Yeah, but nothing compared to you," Juan replied, taking her hand and pulling her a little closer.

Claudia felt her heart race. They were surrounded by people, but in that moment, it felt like there were only the two of them. Juan looked at her with an intensity that left her speechless, and then, gently, he embraced her.

"Claudia, I know we haven't had much time together, but it feels like every moment with you has been special. I don't want to rush anything, but I want you to know that I'm here, for whatever comes next. I want to get to know you more, to share more moments like this with you," he said, his voice steady but filled with emotion.

Claudia looked at him, feeling her eyes fill with tears. There was something so honest in his words, so genuine, that she couldn't help but smile.

"I want that too, Juan. I don't know what will happen, but I want to try with you. I want to build something real, something that lasts beyond this Christmas," she replied, feeling every word come straight from her heart.

They stood in silence for a moment, holding each other under the tree's lights while the Christmas music enveloped them. For Claudia, that moment was perfect, a memory she knew she would keep forever.

After a while, they decided to head back. Juan walked her to the door of her apartment, strolling through the quiet, snowy streets. When they arrived, they both knew they didn't want to say goodbye, but they also understood that it was important to let things unfold at their own pace.

"Thank you for tonight, Juan. It's been… perfect," Claudia said, looking at him with a mixture of gratitude and affection.

"Thank you, Claudia. It's been perfect because I was with you," he replied, leaning in to kiss her on the cheek.

As Juan walked away, Claudia watched him until he disappeared around the corner. Then she entered her apartment, feeling like everything in her life had changed. She turned on the lights of the Christmas tree and sat down on the couch, holding the wooden star he had given her.

She knew she was at the beginning of something new, something that filled her with hope and joy. Christmas was just a few days away, and for the first time in a long time, Claudia felt excited about what was to come.

December 15

The shy December sun softly illuminated Claudia's apartment as she lay under the blankets, reflecting on the events of the past few days. It had been an intense week. Since her date with Juan on December 9th, every moment with him had been a whirlwind of emotions. But just as the magic she felt when they were together was undeniable, a small voice had started to whisper in her mind: "Are you moving too fast?"

Claudia sighed, gazing at the twinkling lights on her Christmas tree in the living room. She wasn't the only one asking herself that question—her friends had hinted at it too. The night before, during a brief meeting at the office, Laura, her best friend, had expressed her concerns.

"Claudia, I get that Juan seems perfect, but… don't you worry it's too soon to be this sure?" she had asked as they were leaving the building.

"It's not that I'm sure, Laura. It's just that when I'm with him, everything feels like it makes sense," Claudia had replied, her voice a mix of conviction and doubt.

Laura had raised an eyebrow but hadn't pushed further. Now, in the quiet of her apartment, her friend's words echoed in her mind. Maybe she was being impulsive; maybe she should keep her mind open and continue exploring before getting emotionally involved. But, on the other hand, wasn't that the point of her challenge? To find someone she truly connected with before Christmas?

To clear her head, Claudia decided to call her friends Laura and Sofía for a coffee. They agreed to meet at a small café they often frequented—a cozy spot with minimalist Christmas decorations and the constant aroma of freshly baked pastries.

Laura and Sofía arrived almost at the same time, both bundled up in thick jackets and colorful scarves that stood out against the cold gray of the city.

"Claudia!" Sofía exclaimed, giving her a hug. "How was the Christmas market with Juan? I need all the details!"

Claudia smiled and began recounting the date, from the stalls they visited to the wooden star ornament Juan had bought for her. As she spoke, her friends listened attentively, but Claudia couldn't help but notice the look on Laura's face—the one she always wore when she was about to offer a critical opinion.

"So, do you feel... sure?" Laura finally asked, stirring her coffee with a spoon.

"Sure of what?" Claudia responded, though she knew exactly what Laura meant.

"Sure that you're not idealizing everything. I mean, you've been with Juan for less than a week, and while he seems charming, how can you know this is real?" Laura pressed.

"I get your concern, Laura, but... some things just feel right," Claudia said, trying to explain something she didn't even fully understand herself. "With Juan, I don't feel like I need time to decide if he's the right one. Everything just fits."

Sofía, who had been listening quietly, chimed in:

"I think you should trust your instincts, Claudia. Sure, it might be fast, but maybe it's the right time. We can't always plan how things happen."

Sofía's words brought Claudia some comfort, but the doubts lingered, like a persistent echo in her mind. After coffee, as she walked home, Claudia decided there was only one way to resolve it: by facing her fears and listening to her heart.

That afternoon, Claudia decided to send Juan a message. She wanted to see him, talk about her doubts, and share her feelings openly. She wrote:

"Hi, Juan. Do you have time for a coffee this afternoon? I'd love to see you and talk."

Juan replied almost immediately:

"Of course, Claudia. How about 5 o'clock at La Posada del Café?"

Claudia felt a wave of relief when she saw his response. She got ready carefully, choosing a casual yet nice outfit, and headed to the café. The cold air cleared her mind as she walked, and when she arrived, she saw Juan waiting by the window. His warm, genuine smile immediately put her at ease.

"Hi, Claudia. How's everything?" he asked when they sat down, noticing the seriousness in her expression.

"Yeah, well… actually, I wanted to talk to you because there's something that's been on my mind," she said, trying to sound calm.

Juan nodded, listening attentively, and Claudia began to explain.

"I know this is new for both of us, and I know we're just getting to know each other. But… I can't help but think everything is happening so fast. I've heard comments from my friends, and while I know how I feel, sometimes I wonder if I'm being impulsive," she confessed, feeling a weight lift off her shoulders as she said it out loud.

Juan looked at her calmly, letting her finish before responding.

"Claudia, I completely understand what you're saying. And, to be honest, I've thought about that too. It's not common to feel such a strong connection with someone so quickly, but I think that's what makes it special. I don't want to rush you or pressure you, but I want you to know that I'm here because I believe in what we're building. If you need time, I get it. But if you decide to move forward, I want you to know I'm with you, no matter what."

Juan's words were exactly what Claudia needed to hear. She had feared that he might take her doubts as a rejection, but instead, he had shown patience and understanding. She realized that those same qualities were what had drawn her to him from the beginning.

"Thank you, Juan. I think I needed to hear that to realize I'm exactly where I want to be. Maybe it's fast, but I don't want to ignore how I feel. I want to move forward with you," she said, taking his hand across the table.

Juan smiled, squeezing her hand warmly.

"Then let's move forward together. At our own pace, no rush, but with open hearts," he replied.

After coffee, they decided to take a walk in a nearby park, which was covered in snow and decorated with Christmas lights. They strolled slowly, enjoying the fresh air and each other's company. They talked about everything and nothing, laughing and sharing anecdotes from their lives, as if the doubts had melted away.

When they reached a small bridge lit by lanterns, Juan stopped and looked at Claudia.

"You know, this is one of my favorite spots in the city. I always come here when I need to clear my mind. I think it's perfect that we're here now," he said, looking at her with tenderness.

Claudia smiled, feeling her fears disappear completely. She stepped closer to him and hugged him, letting the warmth of his body envelop her.

"Thank you for being so patient with me, Juan. I can't promise I won't have doubts again, but I can promise I'll try, because I believe in what we're building," she said.

Juan hugged her tighter, and in that moment, under the lights of the bridge and surrounded by the stillness of the snowy park, Claudia knew she had made the right choice.

Doubts and fears would always appear, but what mattered was facing them together, with honesty and trust. And that's exactly what they were doing.

December 16

The morning of December 16 dawned cold, with the air thick with humidity, promising more snow in the coming hours. Claudia woke up early, feeling lighter than in the past few days. Her conversation with Juan the previous evening had cleared away many of her doubts, and now she was determined to give her best to build something real with him. However, there was still one truth she had to confess to him, something she had kept hidden until now: the advent calendar she had created to find love before Christmas.

From the beginning, it had been a personal project, a way to challenge herself to step out of her comfort zone. But now, with Juan in her life, that "little strategy" felt like too big a secret to keep. If their relationship was going to be honest, as they had both agreed, she had to tell him.

Claudia knew it wouldn't be easy, but she also knew Juan deserved the truth. She decided that tonight, during their date at the café that had become their special place, she would open up completely. She felt nervous, but also confident that he would understand her reasons.

After spending the morning working from home, Claudia decided to go for a walk before her date with Juan. She needed some fresh air to clear her mind. She bundled up in a thick wool sweater and a long coat and stepped into the streets of Madrid, now covered by a light layer of snow. The city had a special glow this time of year, with every corner seeming to be wrapped in the magic of Christmas.

As she walked, she rehearsed in her mind the words she would use to explain her dating calendar to Juan. She wanted him to understand that it hadn't been a game or a way to manipulate anyone, but an honest attempt to find something she had long lost: love.

She stopped in front of a shop window decorated with golden lights and small wooden ornaments. Inside, she saw a handmade heart-shaped pendant carved from olive wood. Something about the little object caught her attention, and she decided to go in and buy it. She thought it would be a symbolic gesture, a reminder for both of them of the honesty and connection they were building.

With the pendant in her bag and a renewed sense of determination, she returned home to get ready for the date.

At six o'clock, Claudia arrived at *La Posada del Café*. The place was livelier than ever, with couples and families enjoying hot drinks and the festive atmosphere. Christmas lights hung from the ceiling, and soft instrumental music filled the air.

Juan was already there, sitting at their usual table by the window, with a cup of coffee in front of him. When he saw her enter, he flashed a smile that made Claudia temporarily forget her nerves. She walked over to him, and he stood up to greet her with a kiss on the cheek.

"Hi, Claudia. You look beautiful," he said as they both sat down.

"Thanks, Juan. You too. How's your day been?" she asked, trying to sound relaxed.

The first few minutes passed with small talk: work, the weather, Christmas plans. But Claudia knew she couldn't postpone the conversation she had in mind. After a few sips of her café con leche, she took a deep breath and looked Juan directly in the eyes.

"Juan, there's something I need to tell you," she began, setting her cup down and folding her hands in her lap. "Something I haven't told you yet, but I feel it's important that you know."

Juan furrowed his brow slightly, but his gaze remained warm and receptive.

"Tell me, Claudia. I'm here to listen," he replied.

Claudia took a deep breath, feeling her heart race.

"When I met you, I was in the middle of a personal challenge I set for myself this December. I called it my 'advent calendar of love.' The idea was to have a different date every day until Christmas, as a way of stepping out of my comfort zone and maybe finding someone special to share the holidays with."

She paused to gauge Juan's reaction. He was watching her attentively, not interrupting, which encouraged her to continue.

"When I met you on December 9, you were one of those dates. But something changed for me after that night. I felt like I didn't need to continue with the calendar, but I was so committed to the idea of completing it that I kept going for a few more days. Until I realized I was just looking for an excuse not to admit that what I really wanted was to be with you."

Juan stayed silent for a moment, processing what he had just heard. Claudia felt a knot in her stomach, fearing that her confession might have pushed him away. But then he smiled, a mix of surprise and tenderness in his expression.

"So I was part of an advent calendar?" he asked, chuckling softly. "Well, I have to say, I never thought I'd be part of something so creative."

Claudia let out a nervous laugh, relieved by his response.

"I'm sorry if this surprises or bothers you. That wasn't my intention, but I didn't know how to tell you without it sounding... strange," she said.

Juan shook his head, taking her hand across the table.

"Claudia, thank you for telling me. I understand why you did it, and I don't judge you. In fact, I admire that you dared to do something like that. But what really matters is that you're here now, being honest with me. That means a lot to me."

Claudia felt her eyes well up with tears of relief. All of her fear of losing him melted away in that moment.

After talking, Claudia took the small wooden pendant out of her bag and showed it to Juan.

"I saw this while I was walking this afternoon. I don't know why, but it made me think of us. It's simple, but it has a special meaning. I want you to have it, as a reminder that I'm here, with you, ready to be honest and build something real," she said, handing it to him.

Juan took the pendant carefully, admiring the carved details in the wood. Then he slipped it into the inner pocket of his coat, looking at Claudia with an expression of gratitude and emotion.

"Thank you, Claudia. This means a lot to me. And I want you to know that I'm here, with you, too," he said, leaning in to kiss her gently.

After leaving the café, they decided to take a walk through the snow-covered streets. The night was quiet, with only a few people on the streets and a silence that was only interrupted by the crunch of their footsteps in the snow. They walked hand in hand, talking about their Christmas plans and what they hoped for the future.

"You know? I've never had a Christmas like this before," Claudia said, looking at the lights that decorated the balconies of the buildings.

"How is this Christmas?" Juan asked, looking at her with curiosity.

"Full of hope, of excitement... and the feeling that something good is starting," she replied, smiling.

Juan stopped for a moment and looked her in the eyes.

"I think that's the magic of Christmas. It's not the lights or the gifts, but moments like this, when you realize that everything you need is right in front of you," he said, leaning in to kiss her under the soft glow of a streetlamp.

Claudia felt like the world stopped in that instant, as if the snow, the lights, and the cold disappeared, leaving only the warmth of his kiss and the certainty that she had found something special.

December 17th

The December sun gently illuminated Claudia's apartment, reflecting off the icy windowpanes. It was a Sunday, and the city was wrapped in the stillness typical of a winter's day. Claudia woke up feeling lighter, as if the confession she made to Juan the night before had lifted a weight she hadn't realized she was carrying.

She got up, made a cup of coffee, and turned on the Christmas tree lights. As the aroma of the coffee filled the air, she curled up on the couch, watching the lights twinkle. She was happy, more than she had remembered being in a long time. Juan had reacted in the best possible way to her confession, and the gesture of keeping the pendant in his coat had filled her with hope. *This is working,* she thought, smiling to herself.

However, as she mentally reviewed the coming days, she recalled something she hadn't fully considered: the question still lingered—what would her family think when she told them she was bringing someone to Christmas dinner? The idea of facing her aunts' famous questions and her parents' inquisitive stares slightly disturbed the peace of her morning.

She decided not to dwell on it too much and, instead, began getting ready to go out. There were still some last-minute Christmas shopping errands to run, and she figured it would be a good day to clear her mind.

After spending the morning at the bustling Christmas market, Claudia decided to take a break. The temptation of a hot coffee and the familiar atmosphere of *La Posada del Café* was impossible to ignore. As she entered, she was welcomed by the warmth of the place and the sound of a soft Christmas carol playing in the background.

The place was busy, but Claudia found a table in the corner, near the window. Miguel, the waiter who already knew her usual order, approached with a smile.

"Claudia! What a surprise to see you on a Sunday. Your usual coffee with milk?" he asked, pulling out his notebook.

"Hi, Miguel. Yes, please. And maybe a croissant, to make up for all this cold," she replied, taking off her coat.

As she waited, she looked out the window, watching the snow start to fall again. It was a peaceful moment, almost perfect, until a familiar voice rang out behind her.

"Claudia! What a coincidence to see you here."

She turned around and saw David, her first date from the *Advent Calendar*. Her surprise was immediate, but she managed to keep her composure as he approached with a smile.

"David, hi! What a surprise to run into you here," she said, trying to sound casual.

David was a tall man with light brown hair and warm eyes, with an easy smile that had been pleasant during their date. Although there hadn't been any spark between them, Claudia remembered that their conversation had been smooth and comfortable.

"Mind if I sit?" he asked, pointing to the chair across from her.

"Of course," Claudia replied, although she wasn't sure how this conversation would unfold.

David ordered a coffee and began talking about how busy he'd been over the past few weeks. Claudia, although interested, couldn't help but feel a bit tense. There was something odd about meeting one of her dates now that her life was heading in a completely different direction with Juan.

"You know, I've thought about our date that day. You were really kind, and although it didn't work out between us, I think it was a good moment," David said, smiling sincerely.

Claudia nodded, grateful for his honesty.

"Yes, it was. I think we both realized there was no chemistry, but it was nice to meet you," she responded.

David looked at her for a moment before letting out a soft laugh.

"To be honest, after our date, I met someone. And, well... it worked. We've been seeing each other since then. I thought of you because I feel like that date helped me realize what I was really looking for," he said, a glimmer in his eyes.

Claudia couldn't help but smile. She was happy to hear that, and at the same time, surprised by the coincidence that both of them seemed to have found something special after their encounter.

"That's incredible, David. I'm really glad to hear that. I'm also in an interesting place right now. I met someone, and… well, I'm discovering something I've never felt before," she confessed, surprised at how easy it was to say.

David nodded, with an understanding expression.

"So, we both came out ahead in some way. Life works in mysterious ways, don't you think?" he remarked, raising his cup in a spontaneous toast.

Claudia laughed and raised her cup too.

"Definitely. Christmas seems to have its own way of putting things in order."

When David left, exiting the café with a calm smile, Claudia was left alone with her thoughts. The encounter had been unexpected, but also revealing. It reminded her that everything she had done so far—every date, every decision, even those that seemed like mistakes at the time—had brought her to this point. And now, with Juan in her life, she felt clearer and more certain than ever about what she wanted.

She paid her bill and stepped out into the cold street, letting the snow touch her face. As she walked toward her apartment, she thought about how she would tell Juan about the encounter. It wasn't important, but she wanted to share it with him, because every detail, every little part of her life, now felt like something she wanted to build together with him.

That night, while preparing dinner, her phone vibrated on the kitchen counter. It was a message from Juan.

"Hi, Claudia. How's your day been? I've been thinking about you and how great I feel since we've been together. Can we talk?"

Claudia smiled as she read it and called him right away. Juan's voice, warm and relaxed, made her feel like they were in the same room.

They talked about their days, shared small anecdotes, and made plans for the coming week. Claudia took the opportunity to tell him about her encounter with David.

"It was curious, but it made me realize something important. Every step I've taken, even the dates that seemed pointless at the time, brought me to you. And now I know it was all worth it," she said, feeling how the words flowed naturally.

Juan paused for a moment before responding.

"Claudia, I feel the same. Everything I've gone through, even the disappointments, seems to make sense now that I'm with you. And even though we're just starting, I want you to know that I'm here to stay, if you want that too."

Juan's words filled her with a warmth that wrapped around her completely. For the first time in a long while, Claudia felt at peace with her decisions and the path she had taken.

"I want that, Juan. I want to build something with you," she responded, her voice full of emotion.

That night, while the lights of the Christmas tree softly illuminated her living room, Claudia sat on the couch with a warm cup of tea. She knew the days leading up to Christmas would be intense, but she also knew she was ready to face them with Juan by her side.

The encounter with David, though unexpected, had served to reaffirm what she already felt: she was exactly where she was meant to be. Christmas was approaching, and with it, the promise of a new beginning.

December 18th

December 18th arrived with a certain special air for Claudia. As she checked her work emails and organized her schedule, a notification on her phone caught her attention: a message from Juan.

"Would you like to have dinner at my place tonight? I'd love to cook for you. What do you think?"

Claudia smiled as she read it. There was something intimate and personal about the invitation, and without hesitation, she replied.

"Of course. Can I bring anything?"

"Just your company," he replied almost immediately, adding a smiling emoji. Claudia felt her heart skip a beat. It had been only a few days since their last date, but every moment with Juan felt like opening a new door to a world where everything seemed simpler, warmer, and full of possibilities.

After finishing her workday, Claudia took some time to get ready. She chose a dark green velvet dress that highlighted her eyes and paired it with small gold earrings, giving her an elegant yet understated look. Before leaving, she grabbed a bottle of wine from her pantry; she didn't want to show up empty-handed.

Juan's place wasn't far, and Claudia arrived on time. The building where he lived had an old-world charm, with wrought-iron details on the doors and a small terrace on the first floor adorned with softly blinking Christmas lights.

Juan opened the door with a wide smile, dressed in a white shirt and dark trousers, which perfectly matched the cozy atmosphere he had created. Claudia immediately noticed the scent of spices and herbs wafting from the kitchen.

"Welcome!" he said, leaning in to kiss her on the cheek. "Come in, make yourself at home."

Claudia stepped inside and was immediately impressed by the apartment. He had decorated everything with impeccable taste: a Christmas tree adorned with warm lights, pine garlands around the windows, and a small collection of ceramic houses lit up, forming a little Christmas village on the coffee table.

"It's beautiful, Juan. Your home has so much... personality," Claudia commented, admiring each detail.

"I wanted tonight to be special," he replied, leading her to the dining room, where a small table was set with white ceramic plates, lit candles, and an open bottle of wine.

The conversation flowed naturally as they dined. Juan had prepared a vegetable lasagna that Claudia described as "the best she had ever tasted." They talked about their Christmas traditions, childhood memories, and the little things that made this time of year so special for both of them.

At one point, as they sipped wine and shared a homemade tiramisu Juan had made, the conversation took a more intimate turn.

"Claudia, there's something I want to tell you," he began, putting his fork down and looking her directly in the eyes. "Since I met you, I've felt something I can't ignore. I don't know if it's the magic of Christmas or just the connection we have, but every moment with you makes me want more. I want to know you more, share more things with you. And I want you to know that I'm here for whatever comes next."

Claudia felt her heart race. There was something in the sincerity of his words, in the warmth of his gaze, that made her feel completely secure. She had also been thinking about him constantly, how every interaction with him felt natural and meaningful.

"Juan... I feel the same. Since our first date, everything has been different with you. You make me feel like I'm exactly where I'm supposed to be, and that's something I've never experienced before," she confessed, taking his hand.

Juan smiled and gently squeezed her fingers.

"Then we're on the same page. What we're building is worth it," he said before leaning in to kiss her.

The kiss was soft but filled with emotion. In that moment, under the warm lights of Juan's apartment, Claudia felt like the rest of the world disappeared. It was just the two of them, sharing something that felt so simple and yet so powerful.

After dinner, they moved to the couch, where Juan had set up a blanket and a couple of cushions. They had a final glass of wine while talking about their plans for the coming days. Claudia decided to be honest about the Christmas dinner with her family.

"My parents host a big dinner every year. It's really important to them, and this year… well, I'd love for you to come with me. But I don't want you to feel like it's an obligation," she said, looking at him nervously.

Juan looked at her, a smile spreading across his face.

"I'd love to go, Claudia. If it's important to you, then it's important to me too. Besides, I want to meet the people who are so important in your life," he replied.

Claudia felt a mixture of relief and excitement. She knew that bringing Juan to the dinner was a big step, but she also knew she was ready for it.

When it was time to say goodbye, Juan walked her to the door. Outside, the snow was gently falling, covering the street with a sparkling, silent layer.

"Thank you for coming tonight, Claudia. It's been one of the best nights I've had in a long time," he said, taking her hands in his.

"Thank you, Juan. It's been… perfect," she replied, looking into his eyes.

They kissed goodbye under the snow, and as Claudia walked home, she couldn't stop smiling. That night, as she settled into bed, she thought to herself that she had never felt anything so clear in her life. Juan was everything she had been looking for, and for the first time in a long time, she felt that Christmas truly had a special meaning.

December 19th

December 19th began with a cloudy sky, gray light filtering through the windows of Claudia's apartment. After the magical evening with Juan the night before, she woke up with a mix of excitement and anxiety. The conversation about the Christmas dinner with her family hadn't been spontaneous: she had been thinking for days about how to bring it up to her parents, especially her aunts, who were known to be the most curious and critical members of the family.

As she prepared her first cup of coffee, Claudia mentally ran through the possible scenarios. Her mother, though loving, had always been traditional and reserved when it came to matters of the heart. Her father, on the other hand, was known for cracking jokes and downplaying tense situations, but Claudia wasn't sure how he'd react to the idea of someone she barely knew joining their family dinner.

What worried her most were her aunts: Elena and Patricia. They represented everything Claudia wanted to avoid. She knew them well, with their penchant for interrogations disguised as innocent questions, and their ability to make anyone feel like they were under a spotlight. Their words from last year still echoed in her head: *"So, when are we going to meet your boyfriend? It's about time, don't you think?"*

Claudia sighed. This year, things would be different. She had someone she truly wanted to introduce, but she feared the moment would turn into more of a test than a celebration.

By mid-morning, Claudia decided that the best course of action was to face her worries head-on. She called her mother while preparing a light breakfast, and after the usual pleasantries, she broached the subject cautiously.

"Mom, I wanted to talk to you about Christmas dinner," she began, slicing a piece of bread.

"Of course, sweetie. Is there something special you wanted to mention?" her mother asked, with the calm voice she was known for.

"Well... this year, I'd like to bring someone. His name is Juan, and we've been seeing each other for a few weeks. He's someone really special, and I think it's the right time to introduce him," Claudia said, waiting for a reaction.

There was a brief silence on the other end of the line, which made Claudia even more nervous. Finally, her mother responded.

"That sounds wonderful, Claudia. If you think it's the right time, I'm sure he'll be welcomed. But you know how your aunts are... They might not be the most delicate when asking questions," she warned, her tone becoming a little more serious.

Claudia laughed nervously.

"I know, Mom. But I think Juan can handle it. I just need you and Dad to be on my side, okay?" she asked, hoping for her support.

"We're always on your side, sweetie. Don't worry," her mother assured her, and the warmth in her voice helped calm Claudia's nerves a little.

Later that day, Claudia met with Laura at their favorite café. She needed to talk to someone who knew her well and could offer an outside perspective on the situation. As always, Laura arrived with her energetic vibe, wearing a red scarf that contrasted with her black coat.

"Okay, what's going on? You've got that look, the one you get when you're overthinking everything," Laura said, sitting down across from Claudia with a hot cup of tea.

Claudia sighed and began explaining everything: her decision to invite Juan to the family dinner, her fears about how her aunts would react, and her concern that the evening could turn into an uncomfortable interrogation.

"Look, Claudia. I know your aunts can be... intense, but I also know you can't let that hold you back. If you truly feel that Juan is important to you, then it's worth facing it. Plus, he seems like a pretty charming guy. I'm sure he can handle Elena and Patricia better than you think," Laura said, taking a sip of her tea.

"It's just that I don't want him to feel pressured. It's our first Christmas together, and I don't want him to walk away with the wrong impression of my family," Claudia replied, stirring her coffee absentmindedly.

"Claudia, if Juan is the guy you say he is, he's not going to be scared off by a couple of nosy aunts. Give him a chance. The worst that could happen is they ask some questions, and I'm sure you'll be there to back him up," Laura said, her voice encouraging.

Claudia nodded. Laura was right. She couldn't protect Juan from everything, but she could be by his side to face it together.

That night, Claudia decided to call Juan to talk more about the Christmas dinner. She wanted to make sure he understood what it meant to her and prepare him for what he could expect from her family.

"Hi, Claudia," he said when he answered, his voice warm. "It's so nice to hear from you. How's your day been?"

"Hi, Juan. Pretty good, although... I've been thinking a lot about Christmas dinner," she replied, sitting on the couch and adjusting her scarf.

"Any particular concerns?" he asked, sensing the tone in her voice.

Claudia laughed softly, trying to ease the tension.

"Let's just say my family isn't exactly straightforward. My mom is sweet, and my dad is laid-back, but my aunts... well, let's just say they can be quite curious. I don't want you to feel uncomfortable or think I'm putting you in a tough situation," she explained.

Juan chuckled softly on the other end of the line.

"Claudia, thanks for telling me, but don't worry. I'm ready for anything. Plus, I want to be there with you. If that means answering some uncomfortable questions, I'll do it happily," he said, with a sincerity that made Claudia feel more at ease.

"Thanks, Juan. That means a lot to me. I promise I'll be by your side the whole time," she said, feeling a wave of gratitude.

With the conversation with Juan settled, Claudia spent the rest of the evening planning how to introduce him to her family. She decided it would be best to arrive a little earlier than the official time, so he'd have a chance to meet her parents in a more relaxed setting before facing her aunts.

She also carefully chose what to bring to the dinner. A homemade Christmas dessert would be a thoughtful gesture and a way to show her family that she had put effort into the evening.

As she prepared the ingredients for a yule log filled with hazelnut cream, she felt her nerves gradually dissipating. She was excited, and although she knew the night would be a challenge, she also knew it would be worth it.

At the end of the day, Claudia sat by the Christmas tree, watching the lights flicker softly. She had a book in her hands, but she hadn't turned the first page. Her mind was full of thoughts about the upcoming dinner, about Juan, and about how much her life had changed in the past few weeks.

She smiled, letting the weight of her doubts disappear. For the first time in a long while, she felt like she was exactly where she needed to be. And although she knew the dinner with her family would be a challenge, she also knew she was ready to face it with Juan by her side.

December 20th

December 20th dawned with a sky covered in clouds, signaling a possible snowfall. Claudia woke up feeling a strange mix of excitement and tension. Christmas was only a few days away, and everything in her life seemed to be moving too fast. On one hand, there was Juan, with whom things felt almost magical. On the other, fears and doubts were starting to creep in.

After breakfast, she decided to go through some pending work cases. Though she was in a more relaxed period before the holidays, she wanted to get ahead of as much as possible so she could fully disconnect during the festive days. However, her mind kept drifting back to Christmas dinner, her conversation with her parents, and especially Juan.

"Is it too soon to bring him to such an important family dinner?" she thought. Her friends' words and her own insecurities were beginning to weigh on her, and she knew she had to address those feelings before they became a problem.

While working, her phone vibrated on the table. It was a message from Juan.

"Good morning, Claudia. I've been thinking… How about we meet this afternoon? I have something on my mind, and I'd love to talk to you about it."

The message took her by surprise. Her heart raced, but she also felt a slight pang of anxiety. She wasn't sure what Juan wanted to talk about, but she knew she couldn't avoid the conversation. She quickly replied:

"Of course, what time works for you?"

"How about 5 o'clock at our café, as usual?"

Claudia sighed, set her phone down on the table, and tried to focus on her work, but the anticipation of her conversation with Juan distracted her. She knew she had to be honest with him about her fears, but she also feared how he might react.

At five o'clock, Claudia arrived at La Posada del Café. The place was bustling as usual, with customers enjoying hot drinks and the festive atmosphere. Juan was already there, sitting at his usual table by the window. When he saw her enter, he smiled, but Claudia noticed a slight trace of seriousness in his eyes.

"Hello, Claudia," he said, standing to greet her with a kiss on the cheek. "I'm glad you could make it."

"Hi, Juan. Of course, I couldn't miss our date," she replied, trying to sound casual.

They ordered their drinks, and for the first few minutes, they chatted lightly about their days and plans for the week. However, Claudia could feel that Juan had something on his mind, something that didn't take long to surface.

"Claudia, I want to talk to you about something that's been on my mind," he began, setting his coffee cup down on the table. "Don't get me wrong, but I feel like everything is moving really fast. What I feel for you is real, but I also feel like we're moving ahead without stopping to breathe."

Claudia felt her heart sink a little upon hearing those words. She had been worried about the same thing, but hearing Juan express it made her feel vulnerable.

"I understand what you're saying, Juan. I've been thinking about it too. It's just that… when I'm with you, everything makes sense, but at the same time, I sometimes wonder if I'm rushing things," she confessed, staring at her cup.

Juan nodded, his expression calm, yet his thoughts were clearly intense.

"I'm not saying I don't want to move forward with you, Claudia. What I want is for us to take it slow, making sure every step is the right one. I want this to work, but I want to do it the right way," he said, reaching across the table to take her hand.

Claudia looked at him, feeling a mix of relief and sadness. She knew Juan was right, but she also feared that "taking it slow" could mean distancing themselves.

"I agree, Juan. The last thing I want is for something to go wrong between us. I just… I don't want to lose what we have," she said, her voice breaking slightly.

Juan gently squeezed her hand.

"You're not going to lose me, Claudia. What we're building is important to me, and I want it to grow solidly. If we need some space to think, I think that will do us good," he replied.

After they said their goodbyes, Claudia walked back to her apartment, feeling the night's chill intensify with each step. Her thoughts were a whirlwind of conflicting emotions: sadness, relief, fear.

When she arrived home, she took off her coat and sat next to the Christmas tree, watching the lights twinkle. Everything had been going so well with Juan, and now she felt like the first conflict between them could change everything.

"Is this a step forward or a step back?" she wondered, gently stroking the wooden pendant Juan had given her. She remembered his words: "I'm here for whatever comes." She decided to hold onto that thought. Maybe this wasn't the end, but simply an obstacle they had to overcome together.

As she mentally replayed the conversation, her phone rang. It was Laura.

"Claudia, is everything okay?" her friend asked, noticing the tension in her voice.

Claudia told her everything about the talk with Juan, from her fears to the decision to take some time to reflect.

"Claudia, I know this scares you, but sometimes conflicts are necessary. If you both are willing to work through it, this can make you stronger," Laura said, always straightforward.

"I hope so, Laura. The last thing I want is to lose him," Claudia replied, feeling a lump in her throat.

"You won't lose him, my friend. Trust in what you both feel for each other. You just need to be patient," Laura reassured her.

That night, Claudia went to bed early, but sleep didn't come easily. Her thoughts kept returning to Juan, his words, and the promise not to give up. Looking at the shadows of the Christmas lights on the ceiling, she decided that, even though this conflict scared her, she was willing to fight for what she had with him.

December 21st

December 21st dawned with a biting chill, but the cold outside couldn't compare to the unease Claudia felt inside since her conversation with Juan. She had spent the night in a state of sleeplessness, thinking about what it meant to "take things slow." It wasn't a breakup, but the simple fact that Juan had felt the need to bring it up had stirred her deepest insecurities.

As she sipped her first cup of coffee by the window, she gazed out at the snow-covered streets. Christmas was only a few days away, and despite the magical atmosphere surrounding her, in her heart there was an echo of doubt. She decided she couldn't stay at home lost in her thoughts. She needed clarity, and perhaps talking to someone she trusted would help her clear her mind.

Without hesitation, Claudia called Laura, her trusted friend and confidante through thick and thin. Laura, as usual, didn't hesitate to invite her for breakfast.

"I knew you'd call. Want me to pick you up in half an hour?" Laura asked as soon as she answered.

"Do you know me that well?" Claudia responded with a half-laugh.

"It's my job as your best friend. Plus, something tells me this has to do with Juan, am I right?"

"Let's just say... you'll need a lot of details to understand everything," Claudia sighed.

Half an hour later, they were sitting in a cozy café nearby. Laura wore a red hat that matched her scarf, and her positive energy was the perfect contrast to the anxiety Claudia exuded.

"Alright, spill it. What happened?" Laura asked as she stirred the sugar into her cappuccino.

Claudia told her everything: how they had discussed the pace of their relationship, how Juan had expressed his concern about moving too quickly, and how she had felt on the edge of losing what they were building.

"I don't think it was a fight, but it wasn't a conversation that left me feeling calm either. I don't want this to turn into a pause disguised as 'time to think,'" Claudia said, dropping her spoon onto the empty plate.

Laura nodded, listening attentively.

"Claudia, I understand your fear, but from what you're telling me, it doesn't sound like he wants to distance himself. It sounds more like he wants what you have to last and be solid. What you said about not wanting to lose him... I think you should stop seeing it as a possibility and start seeing it as an opportunity to show him you're ready to build something real," Laura said, her usual practical tone taking over.

"And how do I do that without seeming desperate?" Claudia asked, furrowing her brow.

"Just be yourself. Talk to him. Tell him how you feel, and, most importantly, listen. I think the core of all this is that you're both navigating something new, and it's normal for there to be moments of doubt," Laura concluded.

Claudia knew her friend was right. The only way to clarify her feelings was to speak directly with Juan.

Back at her apartment, Claudia sat by the Christmas tree, watching the lights flicker as she tried to gather the courage to text Juan. She knew she needed to talk to him, but she feared her own insecurities might betray her.

Finally, she picked up her phone and wrote:

"Hey Juan, I've been thinking a lot about our conversation. I'd like to see you to talk more if you're free today."

She didn't have to wait long for a reply.

"Of course, Claudia. I've been thinking about us too. How about 5 pm at our café?"

Claudia sighed as she read the message. There was something reassuring about how Juan always stayed calm, even when things seemed complicated. She decided this would be the perfect opportunity to be honest and clear the air between them.

At five o'clock, Claudia arrived at La Posada del Café. The place was as cozy as always, filled with couples and friends enjoying the festive atmosphere. Juan was already sitting at their usual table by the window, with a cup of coffee in front of him and a serene expression that made Claudia feel a little less nervous.

"Hey, Claudia," he said, standing up to greet her with a kiss on the cheek. "I'm glad you came."

"Hi, Juan. Thanks for making the time," she replied, sitting down across from him.

They ordered their drinks, but the light conversation that followed was just a prelude to what they both knew they needed to discuss. Finally, Claudia took a deep breath and decided to be the first to bring it up.

"Juan, I want to thank you for what you said yesterday. I know it wasn't easy for you to be so honest, and I think that shows how much you care about what we're building," she began, looking down at her coffee cup. "But I also want you to know that I was scared. Not because I doubt you or us, but because I realized how much you mean to me."

Juan listened carefully, his expression calm but intense.

"Claudia, I understand how you feel. And I want you to know that everything I said yesterday was because I want what we have to be real and lasting. I don't want to rush it, but I also don't want you to think I have doubts about what I feel for you," he said, taking her hand across the table.

Claudia felt her heart calm as she heard his words. The warmth of his touch and the sincerity in his voice made her realize that they had overcome this hurdle together.

"Thank you, Juan. I think we were both projecting our insecurities, but now I know we can get through this if we keep being honest with each other," she replied, squeezing his hand.

Juan smiled, and at that moment, Claudia knew everything would be okay.

After finishing their drinks, they decided to take a walk through the snow-covered streets of Madrid. The snow was falling gently, creating a magical atmosphere as they walked hand in hand. The cold air made the warmth of their bodies together even more comforting.

"I was thinking about the Christmas dinner with your family," Juan said, breaking the silence.

"And what do you think?" Claudia asked, curious.

"I want to go. I know it's important to you, and I want to get to know you more through the people you love. Plus, I like challenges," he replied with a playful smile.

Claudia laughed, relieved by his response.

"Thank you, Juan. That means a lot to me. I promise it won't be as terrible as you think... or at least, I hope not," she joked.

They both laughed, and the weight of the previous days seemed to melt away completely.

They stopped at a small square where a giant Christmas tree sparkled with golden lights. Juan turned to Claudia, with a serious but warm expression.

"Claudia, I want you to know something. No matter what happens, I'm here for you. What we're building is important to me, and I want it to last. I know it won't always be easy, but I'm willing to try," he said, cupping her face in his hands.

Claudia felt her eyes well up with tears, but this time, they were tears of happiness.

"I want that too, Juan. I want this to work, because what I feel for you is different from anything I've felt before," she replied before leaning in to kiss him.

The kiss was gentle and full of emotion, and in that moment, under the lights of the tree and surrounded by snow, Claudia knew they had overcome an important obstacle. What they had was real, and they were both committed to making it work.

That night, as she returned home, Claudia sat by her Christmas tree with a cup of hot tea. She watched the lights flicker and recalled every moment of her day with Juan. Despite the fears and doubts, she felt more certain than ever that she was exactly where she needed to be. Christmas was just around the corner, and for the first time in a long time, Claudia felt completely at peace.

December 22

December 22nd began with a clear sky and the crisp winter air typical of Madrid. Claudia woke up feeling lighter than in the past few days. Her reconciliation with Juan had dispelled her fears, and now there was only one thing left to do: prepare for the big night—the Christmas dinner with her family.

As she stretched in bed, a ray of light came through the window, illuminating the lights on her Christmas tree. Claudia smiled as she remembered Juan's words from their walk the night before: "I'm here for whatever comes." That certainty gave her the strength to face anything, even the inevitable questions from her aunts.

She got up with energy and made herself a cup of coffee, mentally ticking off a list of things to do before the dinner. She knew time would fly, and she wanted everything to be perfect.

After breakfast and a quick check of some work emails, Claudia bundled up and headed to the Christmas market. She wanted to find a special gift for each member of her family, something that reflected the spirit of the season. She also planned to find something for Juan, though she knew he didn't expect anything other than her company.

The market was bustling with life: families strolling through the stalls, children laughing as they pointed at toys, and the air was filled with the scent of roasted chestnuts and holiday sweets. Claudia lost herself in the bustle, wandering through the stalls in search of something that caught her eye.

At a craft booth, she found a small hand-painted wooden box decorated with holiday motifs. She thought it would be perfect for her mother, who always kept little trinkets in her dresser. For her father, she picked out a gardening tool set, a hobby he had recently taken up.

As she paid, her thoughts turned to Juan. "What could I get him? He seems to have everything," she wondered. She continued exploring the market until she came across a small booth selling antique books. There, a volume on architecture caught her eye: *The Secrets Behind the Great Cathedrals.* She thought it would be the perfect gift, given Juan's passion for his work.

Back home, Claudia set to work preparing the dessert she would bring to dinner: a Yule log filled with hazelnut cream and covered in chocolate. It was a recipe she had learned from her mother years ago, and she knew it was always a hit with her family.

As she mixed the ingredients, she played some Christmas music to lift her spirits. Her kitchen soon filled with the sweet scent of the cake baking, and Claudia couldn't help but feel proud of her work. "This is going to be a hit," she thought as she dusted powdered sugar over the finished dessert.

She took advantage of the remaining time to carefully wrap the gifts, choosing bright wrapping paper and golden ribbons. She paid special attention to wrapping Juan's gift, imagining his reaction when he opened it.

As she finished placing the gifts under the tree, her phone buzzed on the table. It was a message from Juan:

"Hey, Claudia. I've been thinking about you all day. Would you like me to come over this afternoon? I have something for you."

Claudia felt a mix of surprise and excitement. She hadn't expected to see him until the Christmas dinner, but the idea of spending time with him before the big night filled her with joy.

"Of course. How about 5? I've got hot coffee and a dessert you might want to try," she replied with a smile.

At five o'clock, Juan arrived at Claudia's apartment, carrying a small gift bag. He was dressed in a dark coat and a gray scarf, and as he entered, his smile lit up the room.

"This place smells amazing," he commented, setting the bag on the table and kissing her on the cheek.

"It's my superpower," Claudia joked, leading him to the kitchen where the coffee was already served.

They sat together at the table, enjoying the dessert Claudia had prepared. As they talked about the plans for Christmas dinner, Juan handed her the gift bag.

"This is for you. I wanted you to have it before dinner with your family," he said, his expression a mix of nervousness and excitement.

Claudia carefully opened the package, revealing a small wooden frame with a photograph they had taken together at the Christmas market a few days earlier. The picture captured a moment of pure happiness, and Claudia felt her eyes fill with tears.

"Juan, it's beautiful. Thank you. This means so much to me," she said, hugging him tightly.

"I knew this was the perfect gift because it reflects how I feel about you: happy and at peace," he replied, kissing her gently on the forehead.

As they finished their coffee, Claudia decided to address something that had been on her mind.

"Juan, about the dinner with my family... I want you to know it's not going to be easy. My mom and dad are lovely, but my aunts can be... intense. They're obsessed with knowing everything about my love life, and they'll probably ask you a million questions," she warned, with a nervous smile.

Juan chuckled softly.

"Don't worry, Claudia. I'm ready for anything. Honestly, I'm more nervous about making a good impression on your parents than I am about your aunts," he confessed.

"My parents are going to love you, I'm sure of it. Just be yourself, and everything will be fine," she reassured him, taking his hand to comfort him.

After finishing their coffee, they decided to take a walk through the nearby streets. Snow was beginning to fall again, and the Christmas lights lit up the sidewalks with a warm glow. They walked hand in hand, enjoying the shared silence and the festive atmosphere around them.

At one point, they stopped in front of a small square where a choir was singing Christmas carols. Juan looked at Claudia with a tender expression.

"Claudia, I want you to know that I'm grateful to have found you. This December has been one of the best months of my life, and it's because of you," he said, gently stroking her face.

Claudia felt her heart swell with emotion. No one had ever spoken to her with such sincerity.

"I'm grateful too, Juan. Being with you has made this Christmas different from any other. And I know this is just the beginning," she replied, before leaning in to kiss him.

When they returned to the apartment, they shared a long, warm hug before saying goodbye. Claudia watched Juan walk away, feeling that each day they spent together strengthened what they were building.

That night, as she prepared for bed, she looked at the wooden frame Juan had given her and smiled. She knew the dinner with her family would be a challenge, but she also knew that with Juan by her side, everything would be easier.

Christmas was near, and Claudia felt more prepared than ever to share it with the people she loved.

December 23rd

The morning of December 23rd arrived with a sky covered by thick clouds, promising more snow. Claudia woke up early, driven by a mix of nervousness and excitement. The next day would be the big Christmas dinner with her family, and not only did she need to make sure everything was perfect, but she also had to prepare Juan emotionally for the barrage of questions, comments, and jokes he would inevitably face.

As she made her coffee, Claudia mentally reviewed her to-do list: make sure the gifts were organized, check that the Yule log she had made the day before was just right, and stop by her parents' house to finalize the last details with her mom. Everything had to go perfectly.

She glanced at her phone. There was a message from Juan.

"Good morning, Claudia. I hope you slept well. How about we meet tonight to talk before the big dinner? I want to make sure everything's okay with you."

She smiled as she read it. Juan's concern for her always helped calm her nerves.

"Good morning. Sure, I'd love to see you. How about 6 p.m. at my place?" she replied, knowing that this conversation would be crucial to align their expectations before the big night.

By mid-morning, Claudia gathered the gifts and the dessert she had prepared and headed to her parents' house. Upon arrival, she was greeted by the familiar scent of cinnamon and pine that always filled the air during Christmas at her home. Her mom was in the kitchen, as expected, preparing the main dishes for the following day's dinner.

"Claudia! It's so good that you arrived early. I need your help with the ham glaze," her mother said, handing her an apron and pointing to the ingredients on the counter.

"Sure, Mom. But first, is Dad here? I want to talk to him about something," Claudia replied as she tied the apron around her waist.

"He's in the garden, fixing some lights that aren't working. You know how he is, obsessed with making everything perfect," her mother said, laughing softly.

Claudia stepped out into the garden, where she found her dad crouched by the hedge, carefully checking a string of Christmas lights.

"Dad!" she called, catching his attention.

"Sweetheart! Right on time. Can you hold this while I check the plug?" he asked, motioning to the lights.

Claudia obeyed and waited for him to finish before broaching the subject that had brought her there.

"Dad, I wanted to talk to you about tomorrow. Well, more specifically, about Juan," she began, feeling a little nervous.

"Ah, yes. The famous Juan. Your mother told me you're bringing him to dinner. Is he ready to face your aunts?" her father asked, a playful smile on his face.

"I hope so. But, Dad, I want to ask you something. I know the aunts are going to bombard him with questions, and I just want to make sure that you and Mom make him feel comfortable. It's important to me," she said, looking at him seriously.

Her father set the lights aside and walked over to her.

"Claudia, if this man means something to you, then he means something to us. Don't worry about us. But your aunts… well, you know how they are. You'll have to prepare him for what's coming," he said, giving her a reassuring hug.

Back in the kitchen, Claudia helped her mother with the final preparations while they talked about the dinner and the last-minute details. Between laughter and memories of past Christmas dinners, Claudia felt a mix of nostalgia and excitement for what was to come.

"Are you nervous about introducing us to Juan?" her mother asked as she arranged some side dishes on serving trays.

"A little, yes. He's someone special, Mom. And I want you to see him the way I do," Claudia confessed.

Her mother stopped what she was doing and walked over to her, placing a hand on her shoulder.

"Claudia, if he makes you happy, that's all that matters. We're looking forward to meeting him," she said with a reassuring smile.

In the afternoon, Claudia returned to her apartment to organize the gifts and make sure everything was ready for the next day. As she placed the Yule log in a box to transport it, she heard a knock at the door. She wasn't expecting anyone, but when she opened it, she found Laura holding a small box.

"Laura? What are you doing here?" Claudia asked, surprised.

"Well, as your best friend, it's my duty to make sure you don't lose your mind before the big dinner. And I brought this to help," Laura said, handing her the box.

Inside was a gold pendant with a small snowflake in the center. It was simple but beautiful.

"This is for you to wear tomorrow. And to remind you that everything will be fine, no matter what happens," Laura said with a smile.

Claudia felt touched by the gesture and hugged her friend tightly.

"Thank you, Laura. This means a lot to me," she said, feeling her confidence renewed.

At 6 p.m., Juan arrived at Claudia's apartment, carrying a bottle of wine and his usual warm smile. They greeted each other with a hug, and Claudia led him into the living room, where they had prepared coffee and cookies.

"Are you ready for tomorrow?" Juan asked as they sat on the sofa.

"I think so, although I'm a little nervous. I don't want you to feel uncomfortable with my family. I already warned you about my aunts, right?" she replied, joking slightly to ease the tension.

Juan laughed and took her hand.

"Claudia, don't worry about me. I'm ready for anything. Besides, I'm doing this because I want to get to know you better, and your family is part of that," he said, looking at her sincerely.

Claudia felt a wave of gratitude and decided to be completely honest.

"Juan, this Christmas means a lot to me, not just because you'll be there, but because I feel like with you, things are different. I want you to know that I'm committed to this, to you. And no matter what happens tomorrow, I'm happy you're by my side," she confessed.

Juan smiled and leaned toward her.

"Claudia, I feel the same way. And I'm here to stay, no matter how many questions your aunts ask me," he said, before kissing her.

That night, after saying goodbye to Juan, Claudia sat in front of her Christmas tree and looked at the carefully wrapped gifts waiting to be taken to dinner. For the first time in a long time, she felt truly excited about Christmas—not just for the presents or the traditions, but for the people she would share it with.

As the lights flickered gently, she thought about how much her life had changed in the past few weeks. She had started the month with a personal challenge, and now, she was ending it with something much more meaningful: a real, sincere connection full of possibilities.

With a smile on her lips, she turned off the lights and got ready for bed, knowing that Christmas was just around the corner and that the best was yet to come.

December 24

December 24th arrived under a clear blue sky, with the sun reflecting off the snow that covered the streets of Madrid. Claudia woke up early, feeling a mix of excitement and nervousness. It was the day of the big Christmas dinner, and for the first time in years, she wouldn't be attending alone. She had Juan, and that made this Christmas special.

She got up carefully, letting the scent of freshly brewed coffee fill the apartment. She looked at the soft twinkling lights on her Christmas tree and thought about everything that had happened in the past month: the dates, the doubts, the laughter, the confessions, and above all, the love she had started to build with Juan. For the first time in a long while, she felt hopeful, excited, and sure that she was exactly where she needed to be.

As she mentally ran through her to-do list for her parents' house, she received a message from Juan.

"Good morning, Claudia. I can't wait to see you tonight. I'm sure it will be an unforgettable Christmas."

Claudia smiled as she replied, "Good morning, Juan. I can't wait either. I promise it will be a special day. See you tonight."

With every message, every word they shared, she felt her connection to him grow stronger.

After breakfast, Claudia spent the morning on last-minute preparations. She carefully packed the gifts and dessert she was bringing to the dinner, making sure everything was perfect. While she wrapped the final touches, she received a call from Laura.

"Claudia! Ready for the big night?" Laura asked, her usual enthusiasm in her voice.

"Ready, though a little nervous. I just want everything to go well, especially for Juan," Claudia confessed.

"Claudia, relax. If your parents and aunts see how special he is to you, they'll love him. And remember, you're not alone in this. Juan will be by your side," Laura reassured her.

Claudia knew her friend was right. She had come so far, and now it was time to enjoy everything she had built.

By mid-afternoon, Claudia arrived at her parents' house, gifts and the yule log in hand. The house was decorated with lights and garlands, and the aroma of roasted turkey filled the air. Her mother greeted her with a warm hug, followed by her father, who was already making sure everything was in place.

"Ready for tonight?" her father asked with a knowing smile.

"More or less. I just hope my aunts don't overwhelm Juan too much," Claudia replied as she placed the gifts under the tree.

"Oh, I'm sure he can handle it. If he's made it this far, he's worth it," her father said, giving her a wink.

At nine o'clock, the doorbell rang. Claudia felt her heart race as she walked toward the door. When she opened it, she saw Juan standing there, wearing a black coat and a gray scarf, holding a carefully wrapped box.

"Hello!" he said, his smile immediately calming Claudia's nerves.

"Hi! Come on in," she responded, opening the door wider.

Juan entered, greeting Claudia's parents with warmth. After a few minutes of introductory conversation, it was time to face the rest of the family. Aunts Elena and Patricia were in the living room, already with their glasses of wine and curious looks.

"So, this is Juan!" Elena exclaimed, moving forward to shake his hand. "Tell us, how did you meet our Claudia?"

Claudia rolled her eyes discreetly, but Juan, keeping his composure, replied with a smile.

"We met in a place that's become very special to us. From the very beginning, I knew Claudia was someone different," he said, gazing at Claudia with tenderness.

The aunts exchanged glances, clearly surprised by his response, but didn't ask any further probing questions. Claudia felt a wave of relief as she saw how Juan handled the situation with confidence and kindness. He even seemed to enjoy sharing stories.

As everyone sat down at the table, dinner proceeded surprisingly smoothly. Claudia's parents made Juan feel right at home, and he charmed them with anecdotes from his work as an architect, showing genuine interest in the family's stories.

"Juan, I must say you have a lot of patience to put up with this family," Claudia's father joked, causing everyone to laugh.

"It's a pleasure to be here. And if I may say so, Claudia has told me a lot about how special this dinner is to all of you. I'm grateful to be a part of it," Juan replied, earning even more points with the guests.

As dessert was served, Claudia looked around the table. Seeing her family laughing with Juan, without any tension or awkwardness, filled her with a warmth she couldn't describe. It was as if everything had fallen into place perfectly.

After dinner, when the family dispersed between conversations and gift exchanges, Claudia and Juan stepped out into the garden to enjoy a quiet moment. The snow continued to fall softly, and the lights on the Christmas tree inside cast a warm glow through the windows.

"How are you feeling?" Claudia asked, looking at him curiously.

"Happy. Your family is wonderful, and tonight has been better than I imagined," Juan replied, taking her hands in his.

"I'm proud of you. I knew you could handle my aunts," Claudia joked, making them both laugh.

Juan moved closer, looking at her with a mixture of affection and determination.

"Claudia, this Christmas is special because I'm with you. I don't know what the future will bring, but I want you to know that I'm ready to face it with you. What we've built so far means a lot to me, and I want to keep building it, step by step, day by day," he said, with a sincerity that made Claudia feel as though time had stopped.

"Juan... I want that too. You've made this Christmas different from any other. With you, everything feels brighter, full of possibilities," she replied, her voice full of emotion.

Under the stars and the gentle falling snow, Juan leaned in and kissed her. It was a kiss full of promises, beginnings, and a love that was just starting but already felt unbreakable.

When they returned inside, they were greeted with laughter and the soft music of Christmas carols. Claudia took Juan's hand, feeling that everything was in its right place. For the first time in years, Christmas wasn't just another tradition; it was the beginning of something real, something worth protecting.

That night, as everyone exchanged gifts and shared stories, Claudia knew that she hadn't just completed her challenge—she had found something far more valuable: love and the promise of a shared future.

And with that, Christmas became a reminder that the most important things aren't planned; they just happen.

Printed in Dunstable, United Kingdom